OUTLAW'S WOMAN

OUTLAW'S WOMAN

BRET REY

A Black Horse Western

ROBERT HALE · LONDON

ISBN 0 7090 5557 9

Robert Hale Limited
Clerkenwell House
Clerkenwell Green
London EC1R 0HT

Photoset in North Wales by
Derek Doyle & Associates, Mold, Clwyd.
Printed and bound in Great Britain by
WBC Book Manufacturers Limited,
Bridgend, Mid-Glamorgan.

For
Tom Moyle
my spiritual mentor

OUTLAW'S WOMAN

ONE

Carl Ranahan felt the muscles of his stomach contracting, recognized the combined feelings of excitement and fear that always flooded through him just before another bank raid. Lips scarcely making any movement, mouth dry, he said to Roy Durwood, riding alongside him, 'I hope Sally got it right this time.'

Durwood slanted a glance at his sidekick. 'When did she ever let us down?'

Ranahan said nothing.

'Well?'

'There's allus a first time.'

'Well until that first time, quit worrying.'

They headed for the Busted Flush saloon, dismounted, hitched their mounts to the tie rail, looked along the length and breadth of the street and, finding nothing to cause them any alarm, turned and pushed into the bar room.

'What'll it be, gents?' the apron asked as they sidled up to the long bar.

'Cool beer,' Ranahan voiced, removing his hat and wiping his brow with a red, white-spotted handkerchief.

Roy Durwood allowed himself to ponder the fear Ranahan had expressed minutes earlier, admitting to himself that one day Sally Freeman might make a mistake. The girl had proved a great asset to the gang since she had quit her home on an Ohio farm to run off with him three years ago. Her beauty and that butter-wouldn't-melt-in-her-mouth look she could put on at will was the secret of her success. Nobody, least of all a bank teller, would ever suspect her of garnering information for a gang of bank robbers. Durwood trusted her, and yet he had no idea what she said to the folks she encountered on her missions, other than what she chose to tell him.

He shrugged, silently upbraiding himself for doubting her as he picked up the beer the apron deposited in front of him, and took a long swig. Hell, but it was hot out there.

The two men drained their glasses and turned

to leave with a nonchalant air, ambling easily towards the door, their brief stay noted, but causing no disquiet to the men who watched their exit.

Outside on the boardwalk they glanced across to the bank, where Arnold Glover and Brian Quarmby had timed their arrival perfectly. Ignoring everyone, just like any men with banking business on their minds, Glover and Quarmby entered the bank.

Durwood and Ranahan strolled leisurely across the street and followed them inside. Glover had taken up a position to the left of the room, while Quarmby had placed himself behind a customer making a deposit, the two men giving the impression that one had business to transact and the other was waiting for him to complete it.

The two newcomers halted in the middle of the room, causing no alarm to the teller, who was busy dealing with his customer. A brief exchange of pleasantries, then the customer swivelled on his heels, nodded to Quarmby, and left with a purposeful stride. Quarmby stepped forward, a small wad of notes in his hand.

'You wish to make a deposit, sir?' the teller queried.

'No, he doesn't,' Durwood said from the rear as the door closed behind the departing customer. 'He's more interested in a withdrawal, and so are we.'

All four men drew their guns and aimed them at the man behind the counter. He raised his hands hurriedly, his face a sudden picture of terror. 'Don't shoot! Don't shoot!' he pleaded in a voice several notches higher than normal.

Alerted by the change in the teller's tone, another man looked up from his desk at the rear, then shot to his feet, equally alarmed, yet defiant.

'Don't be foolish, men. You'll never get away with it. Our town marshal will kill every one of you if you proceed with this attempt at robbery.'

Durwood vaulted over the counter and produced a gunnysack. 'Quit the talking and get that safe door open. Fill this! Pronto!' Ranahan followed him across the polished surface and stood beside the teller.

The banker maintained his defiance, ignoring the gunnysack Durwood held out toward him. 'And if I don't?'

'I'll kill you.' Durwood's voice was softly persuasive. 'Now don't you be foolish.'

On the other side of the counter Glover had moved to lean against the door, in case any other customer attempted to come in just before the bank was due to end the day's business.

'I haven't got all day,' Durwood told the defiant banker, who still hesitated. Durwood knew it couldn't last more than a few seconds. Men with enough acumen to become bankers were not stupid.

The banker fished in a coat pocket and produced a small bunch of keys, then slowly bent to insert one of them in the safe door. It clicked with a double turn and the door opened easily when he pressed the handle in a downward movement. He looked up at Durwood, who tossed the gunnysack to him. Behind them the teller was stuffing notes and silver dollars into another bag with shaking hands, Quarmby's gun pointing threateningly at his head. The teller handed the sack to Quarmby, his eyes wide with fear.

'Now lie down on the floor,' Ranahan instructed.

The man hurriedly obeyed, while Ranahan produced a spare bandanna and used it to gag the teller. Then he tied his hands behind his back with the rope he had brought, using the excess to secure his ankles together.

'That should hold you until your little woman sends somebody to look for you.' He thrust the barrel of his Colt pistol into the back of the teller's neck and said menacingly, 'And when they come to release you, just remember we were all wearing masks, so you don't know what we look like, or we'll be back to make your little woman a widow. Tell your boss that, too, and make sure he understands no town marshal can save him. You got that?'

The teller grunted acquiescence, nodding his head.

Ranahan stood up again, just as the banker held out the filled gunnysack to Durwood, who grabbed it roughly.

'Now gimme those keys!'

The banker passed them over.

'Which one is the door key?'

The banker pointed to the largest of them. 'That one.'

Durwood fingered it free of the others. 'Now turn around.'

The banker was irritatingly slow to obey, which prompted the robber to slug him much harder than he had originally intended. The man slumped unconscious to the floor. It would be a long time before he regained his senses.

The other three men made their way to the door as Glover opened it and stepped out onto the boardwalk. He signalled for them to come out. Durwood closed the door and locked it while the other three shielded him from the view of any interested eyes. Adopting a casual attitude, all four men ambled to their horses and climbed into their saddles. Durwood and Ranahan allowed Quarmby and Glover to go on ahead, to avoid giving the impression all four of them were together. They all walked their horses leisurely out of town so as not to attract undue attention to themselves. It was that time of afternoon when the business community were winding down activities for the day and there were few people on the streets.

Everything had gone according to plan, as usual, except for Durwood having hit the banker too forcefully. He hoped he hadn't killed the man: killing was never a factor in these robberies. Excessive violence had never been necessary and was considered rank foolishness. Quiet, well-planned efficiency was the hallmark of the gang's success. He shrugged away the niggling doubt in his mind.

A mile out of town, Durwood felt his heart sing with an elation he always experienced at such times.

'Let's ride!' he yelled, and spurred his steeldust into a fast gallop.

TWO

Sally Freeman, a mature looking nineteen years old, showed no inkling of nervousness as she waited in the Perrys Hotel, but beneath her well rounded bosom the fear she could never suppress pounded mercilessly. She would be glad when Roy turned up and the anxiety left her. Oak Creek was a long way from the small Texas town selected for this latest heist and it could be well into the next day before he arrived. She had booked them a luxurious double room as Mr and Mrs Freeman. Roy liked a touch of luxury after a raid. It made a nice contrast to the rough and tumble of their general existence with the other three members of

17

Roy's gang, always on the move, sometimes only just ahead of a posse.

As she entered the dining room, eager for supper, she noticed a fair-haired man, tall and handsome, just about to take his seat. He was accompanied by a slim, very attractive Mexican woman, and Sally could not take her eyes off them until her stares attracted their attention. She offered them a smiling nod and then looked away. It still struck her as odd that a Texas man should deign to dine with a Mexican woman. Texans hated Mexicans, or so she had been led to believe. She had no way of knowing that Ralph Coates was not a Texan.

The man was well known in the hotel apparently, judging by the fact that he was on first name terms with the proprietor, who had arrived at their table with a smile of familiarity. Sally Freeman caught the introduction the man made.

'Gilbert, meet Consuela. We met on my mission to New Mexico.'

Gilbert Perry nodded, a half smile on his face, but his manner indicated to the observer that he, too, was a little surprised by the liaison. Sally Freeman was aware that the couple had created more than mere curiosity amongst the other diners as well. In some eyes there was unconcealed hostility.

* * *

The outlaws rode for three hours, then made camp, each man knowing the drill off by heart, each setting about his own task. Arnold Glover produced beans from a sack tied to his saddle horn a coffee pot and a skillet, while Ranahan and Quarmby gathered dry kindling wood. Roy Durwood rustled up some rocks to make a fire stand that would facilitate the means for heating beans and water. Glover ambled down to the creek to fill the coffee pot with fresh water, and replenished his own water bottle at the same time.

Less than an hour later the haul from the robbery was split evenly into five piles, Ranahan, Quarmby and Glover each picking up one pile, leaving the other two for their leader.

Ranahan said, 'You're too generous with that girl, Roy. Giving her all that money'll make her independent.'

Durwood's eyes concentrated hard on his sidekick. 'Keep your nose out of it, Carl. What goes on between me and Sally is none of your business.'

'I'd hate t'see her get you over a barrel, is all.'

'She won't. When are you gonna learn to let your brain get into gear before you open your mouth? Without us she's lost and she knows it, and so should you.'

Durwood turned to the other two. 'Arnold, you

19

take first watch. Wake Brian in two hours. I'm turning in.'

While the others bedded down, Glover went to check on the horses. Satisfied that they were standing quietly, he wandered in a circle around the camp, ears tuned for the sound of anything other than what he would expect to hear at night. Nothing. He was aware that sound travels further in the stillness of night and the absence of hoofbeats confirmed what they had all surmised – no posse was on their tail. It could have been as much as two hours before anybody investigated why the banker and his teller had not returned to their homes.

Glover returned to the fire and huddled deeper into his thick coat. He hated these night watches. After the heat of day he could never understand how it could get so damned cold at night.

Morning arrived and Sally Freeman was not in the best of moods. She had tossed and turned for most of the night and what little sleep she had been able to get was not the kind that left her refreshed. Where were the men now? Had the raid gone well? Did they get away without any gunplay? The questions pounded in her head.

At the breakfast table she drank coffee but ate little. She had been late coming downstairs and there was no sign of the Mexican woman and her tall, handsome companion. Idly she wondered if they had left the hotel together or gone their separate ways. What did it matter to her?

She hated these long waits and wished she was still playing a part in the actual robberies, as she had once in the early days with Roy. The thrill of taking part had always outweighed any fears of capture or getting shot. She decided to explore the town again, which she already knew like the back of her hand. It was something to do.

As she stood outside the bank her thinkbox began to ponder the possibilities. Roy had said it was too risky in view of the fact that another gang had gotten away with a lot of money a few years back, but Sally figured memories would have faded by now. But then she realised Roy would never contemplate raiding a bank in a town where he had become known, if only to a few of the residents. After two days and nights luxuriating in the Perrys Hotel he would be easily recognizable. She passed on and continued her stroll.

'There they go,' the elderly man said. 'Back to that homestead, I guess.'

'You want we should teach him a lesson, Mr Veldon?' Lou Pike asked with a malevolent grin of anticipation.

'You think you can manage that, Lou, without me supervising?'

'You know me, boss. Nothin' I'd like better. If there's anything I hate it's Mex lovers.'

'Wait 'til tomorrow.' The old man's eyes were cold beneath greying brows. He stroked his white moustache caressingly, knowing instinctively that Ralph Coates would be more dead than alive by the time Lou Pike had finished with him. 'Go early, when he'll least expect visitors. And when you've finished with him, leave a warning to anybody passing by. We have to make it clear there's no forgetting the Alamo.'

'We'll do that, Mr Veldon. Come on boys, time to go an' make plans.'

The long-haired Keith Tweedy and his smiling companion, Fred Daly, turned and followed their natural leader.

They arrived just before dawn, having left their mounts a quarter mile away and completed the trek to the house on foot, spurs removed and housed temporarily in their saddlebags.

'Reckon he'll need the privy any time now,' Lou Pike whispered.

In spite of his confidence, Pike became irritable as the men waited in the stables for Ralph Coates to make an appearance.

'What in hell's keepin' him!'

'Reckon he enjoys cuddlin' up to that little Mex woman,' Fred Daly commented. 'You gotta admit she's right pretty, Lou.'

'She's a Mex! Somethin' wrong with a man who'll bed a Mex woman, Fred.'

'I guess so, Lou.'

They had been waiting close to a half hour before the back door of the timber house opened and the tall, blond man appeared, hatless and without his gunbelt.

'He's comin', Lou,' Keith Tweedy announced.

'Yeah. Remember now, we get him when he comes out o' the privy, but don't take any chances. He's a big man an' he ain't gonna give in without a fight.'

'I'll lay him out with one punch,' Fred Daly boasted.

'I'm not so sure about that, Fred. He's a very fit man. It'll take the both of you to get the better of him.'

They watched Coates enter the box type privy, then tip-toed towards it, taking up positions opposite the door, forming a close trio just outside. When the door opened and a dull-eyed Coates emerged, Daly threw a haymaker right that caught him unawares. He tumbled back against the door frame and before he could regain his balance, both Daly and Tweedy hammered him with a series of blows that negated his attempts to defend himself. A final punch from Daly floored him and left him in never-never land.

'Get him over to that corral,' Pike commanded.

'I've gotten the rope.'

They stretched out his arms and tied his wrists tightly to the top bar of the corral, just as he regained consciousness. Lou Pike ripped the shirt from his back, handing the bullwhip to Tweedy.

'Make it good, Keith.'

The other two stood back and watched with sadistic delight as Tweedy swung his arm and the whip cut deep into the blond man's flesh, causing him to cry out in pain. Tweedy's arm swung back, then forward again, extracting another gasp of agony. The process was repeated until Tweedy's arm began to grow tired.

'Give the whip to Fred, Keith. Let him have a go.'

Alerted by the crack of the whip, Consuela Martinez came out of the house to see what was happening. When she saw her beloved Ralph fastened to the corral, his bare back a mass of blood, she cried out in horror. Lou Pike drew his gun and shot her three times.

'Die, you Mexican whore!'

She did, with merciful abruptness.

A minute later Pike called a halt to the beating. 'That's enough, Fred. He'll die slowly, once the sun gets up. Now let's find a board an' some paint and write a warnin' for others.'

After ten minutes they surveyed the short message Pike had painted and nailed to the corral. It read simply, 'Mex lover!'

The three men strolled back to their horses, delighted with their early morning's efforts.

'You reckon Mr Veldon'll be pleased with you, Lou?' Fred Daly queried.

A sadistic grin spread Pike's lips wide. 'You want to tell him what we did, Fred?'

'You'll let me, Lou? You'll let me tell him?'

'Sure, Fred, sure. Mr Veldon likes you.'

The three men put their spurs back on and climbed into saddles, heading back to the ranch. At about the time they arrived at the cookhouse for breakfast, Sally Freeman was chiding Roy Durwood to get out of their hotel bed.

'Come on, Roy, I'm hungry.'

He opened his eyes and grinned at her. 'I'm gonna miss these sheets,' he sighed, his mind already on the journey ahead of them.

THREE

Carl Ranahan, Arnold Glover and Brian Quarmby came out of the rooming house in Oak Creek around nine o'clock and headed for the livery stables to pick up their horses. They exchanged no words, each man occupied with his own thoughts. They paid the liveryman and moved out.

Mounted and heading north, Quarmby broke the silence between them. 'You reckon them two are still bouncin' the bed springs?'

'Wouldn't surprise me,' Ranahan said.

But they were both wrong. Roy Durwood was looking out of the bedroom window as the trio rode passed the Perrys Hotel.

'There they go,' Durwood said over his shoulder, knowing Sally would not need telling who 'they' were.

'Good. We should soon catch up with them. Are you ready?'

'Yep.'

He turned and gave her an appraising look. Even in pants and shirt she looked just as good as when she wore one of her expensive gowns, reserved for such occasions as evenings spent in good class hotels. Pride had shone in his eyes last night as Sally's beauty caused heads to turn in the dining room.

Picking up her bag, he led the way down the stairs to the desk, paid the tab, and bade Gilbert Perry a smiling farewell.

'Come again, Mr Freeman.'

Durwood still found the name came unreal to his ears, but he respected Sally's idea of them using her inherited name when they stayed in hotels. It was good sense for them not to use his own. He was well aware of the likelihood that one day he might not get away with his criminal activities and he didn't want Sally involved if ever he was arrested.

They walked side by side to collect their horses. A half hour later they had caught up with the other three members of the gang.

'You boys have a good night?' Durwood queried.

Not as good as you, Quarmby said to himself, but he mouthed, 'I reckon your bed was more comfortable than mine.'

Durwood grinned. 'Bit hard, was it?'

'You could say that.'

'Explore the town, did you?'

'Had a few drinks, didn't we boys,' Ranahan informed him.

'Not too many, I hope.'

Arnold Glover spoke up. 'You know we ain't stupid, Roy.'

Relieved, Durwood lapsed into silence, until they came in sight of a house and stables over to the right of the trail. It was past midday and the sun was hot, the horses beginning to lather up.

'Let's see what shade we can find over yonder,' Durwood said.

'I could sure use some coffee,' Glover mouthed.

They saw the man and his mutilated back before Sally caught sight of the woman lying on the ground. She leapt from her saddle and ran to check on the still form. Blood lay thickly on the woman's dress and Sally had no need to feel for a pulse. She looked up at Durwood. 'She's dead, Roy.'

'I reckon he is, too,' he said, glancing towards Ralph Coates.

'No, he's not,' Ranahan called back. 'Won't be

long though.'

'Wonder who they are.'

'His name is Ralph Coates. Hers is Consuela,' Sally informed them.

Durwood looked surprised. 'How d'you know?'

'They stayed at the hotel, night before last.'

The gruesome sight of the man's back sickened her, but her compassion conquered her revulsion. 'Cut him loose, Carl, and get him into the house. We might be able to save him.'

Ranahan called, 'Give me a hand, Brian. You, too, Arnold.'

The older man produced his knife and cut the ropes fastening Coates' wrists to the top bar of the corral, while the other two supported him, their hands around his upper arms. Ranahan sheathed his knife and took the man's legs.

'Careful with him!' Sally called. 'Don't catch his back.'

She led the way into the house and into the kitchen by the back door. There was a rough, scrubbed table there and she instructed the men to lay Coates belly down. 'There's water here but no fire. Arnold, rustle up some wood and get a fire going. Carl and Brian, find some clean white sheets if you can. We have to clean him up and then get him into a bed.'

'You're wastin' your time, Sally,' Durwood prognosticated. 'He ain't gonna live after a beatin' like that.'

She glared at him. 'If it was you, would you want me to ride away and leave you?'

Her strident question ended the discussion.

'Who could have done such a thing?' she asked no one in particular. 'It's inhuman to whip a man like this.'

She was struggling to overcome her disgust and feelings of nausea.

'The question is, Sal, why?'

The scorn on her face and the harsh tone of her voice as she stared back at him would have shrivelled most men. 'We know why! That board nailed up beside him is plain enough, but whatever he did or did not do, this was too much.'

'I guess these Texicans never forget the Alamo.'

'That was years ago, Roy. Before we were born. It's likely the men who did this weren't even born either. This is hatred handed down from one generation to another. It's insane.'

Durwood shrugged. 'I guess you're right, honey.'

Arnold Glover returned with kindling wood and set about lighting the stove. Ranahan and Quarmby came back into the kitchen with some cotton sheets and held them out to Sally.

'These do?' Quarmby asked.

'Fine. Rip them into wide strips. I'll need some square pieces to swab away all this blood. They've cut him to the bone with their whips.'

31

'Damage like that must've been done with a bullwhip,' Carl opined in disgust. 'I'd like to get hold of men who'd whip a man and then leave him strung up like that in the hot sun.'

'I guess he never realised the extent of the hatred some Texans have for Mexicans,' Quarmby offered. 'Ain't that so, Arnold?'

Glover looked decidedly uncomfortable. 'I guess you're right, Brian. I tell you, this makes me ashamed to be a Texan.'

The others all knew how much Glover abhorred violence in all its forms. They had often wondered how he could ever have set himself outside the law. It was something he never talked about and prying into a man's background too closely was frowned upon. Each had his own dark secrets, kept hidden from the others.

'Bedding a Mexican woman is the worst sin of all, is it, Arnold?' Durwood asked, looking Glover straight in the eyes.

Glover averted his gaze. 'Looks that way.'

Mercifully for the victim he had lost consciousness, probably due to having his bared head under the hot sun as much as the wounds that had been inflicted on him.

'If he pulls through this, he's a better man than any of us,' Carl Ranahan said with feeling.

He lay on his belly in the bed to which they had

carried him. Sally Freeman had decided against bandaging him after she had cleaned away the blood, fearing that cotton cloth would stick to the harsh wounds Ralph Coates had suffered. She was concerned about him catching a chill in the cold of night, so she instructed the men to build a timber frame to lay above him, over which she would place blankets to shield him from the lowered temperature, while still leaving his torn flesh untouched.

None of the men had raised a question concerning this change in their plans. By nightfall they had anticipated being in El Paso, where it had been their intention to stay only one night. They would all feel safer once they crossed the Texas border into New Mexico. Without any of them realizing it was happening, Sally Freeman had taken over leadership of the gang from her common-law husband, and the strength of sympathy for the victim of such terrible violence amongst the others made Roy Durwood keep his fears to himself. He was the only one who seemed to have no anger in him, still convinced Ralph Coates would be dead by morning. It was his one hope of taking command again.

After Sally had found food and cooked supper for them all, Carl Ranahan rested his eyes on her, seeing how weary she had grown with the distress of tending to the wounded man. 'Leave the dishes,

33

Sally,' he said. 'Me and Arnold will see to them. You get some rest.'

'Thanks, Carl. I do feel pooped.'

'We'd best post guard,' Glover suggested nervously. 'Whoever whipped that man may come back to see if he's dead.'

'And one of us better watch over that poor devil, in case he comes to his senses,' Quarmby hinted. 'He could hurt himself some more if there's no one to talk to him.'

Durwood made a decision. 'All right. Sally sleeps; the rest of us take turns, two hours at a time. Carl and Arnold, me and Brian. You two first. Wake us at midnight, Carl. I don't reckon they'll come back before morning, but we can't be sure.'

'Will do. Looks like we'll not be seeing El Paso for a day or two yet.'

There was no mention of what they would do when anyone returned to check on their handi-work, but they all knew without being told that Sally Freeman would not leave until Ralph Coates was either conscious again or dead.

FOUR

It was just before five in the morning that Ralph Coates began to stir. He slipped in and out of consciousness several times before he felt the fierce burning of his torn flesh, and the cries of anguish alerted Roy Durwood to what he had never expected to see. He moved towards the bed. In the dim light of the lantern he noticed the eyes of the mutilated man were open.

Coates' brain began to function. The man looking down on him was a total stranger. 'Who are you?' Coates croaked from a dry mouth.

'Just a passing stranger.'

Wincing with pain, his eyes clamped tight shut,

teeth gritted, Coates attempted to ease his aching limbs.

'Don't!' Durwood cautioned sharply. Then in a more amenable tone, 'You're cut up pretty bad. Stay on your belly. We've rigged you some protection from the bedding. Didn't want to bandage you up and then have it stick to your wounds.'

'It was you ... who found me?'

'Yeah.'

After a short silence Coates mumbled, 'You said "we". Who else?'

'My wife, Sally, and three friends.'

Much as he wanted to shut out the memory of the beating he had taken, the burning pain of his wounds would not let him. He recalled the shots he had heard just before he passed out. Consuela. Where was Consuela?

He raised his eyes to look questioningly at his benefactor. 'There was a ... woman ... here, Con....'

'They shot her. She's dead. One of the boys made a box for her. We plan to bury her this morning, if that's all right with you?'

The prone man dropped his gaze. He was silent for a long time, then he murmured softly, 'Thanks.'

'You rest easy now.'

'I ... could use ... a drink of water.'

'I'll get you some.'

36

Durwood returned with a china cup, half filled. 'Don't roll on your back: just turn enough so you can drink.'

He held the cup to Coates' lips as the man turned on his right side and tilted his head. Coates took a gulp of the water, some of it dribbling down his right cheek. Durwood waited a moment before offering him any more. Same result. Some went down the man's throat and more spilled out of his mouth.

'I reckon that tastes good, huh?'

An almost imperceptible nod, and then Coates lowered his head back to the pillow and closed his eyes again. Durwood left him, unsure whether to be pleased or sorry that Coates had surfaced. With wounds so deep and the agony he would continue to suffer, the man would have been better off dead.

'He must have the constitution of an ox,' Brian Quarmby opined as Sally Freeman came into the kitchen.

She faced Quarmby, ignoring the others. 'He's still alive?'

'And hurting.'

She left the kitchen and hurried to the bedroom where the wounded man had been laid. The intrusion roused him. He eyed the woman as she stood just inside the room, gazing steadily at him, her face a picture of concern.

'Howdy,' he said softly.

She moved towards the bed. 'Hurts bad, does it?'

'Awful.'

Roy Durwood had followed her and stood in the doorway, watching the exchanges.

Sally said, 'They whipped you so much I expect they thought you would die. So did we, but we couldn't ride away and leave you.'

His gaze remained steadily on her. 'Are you....?'

'Yes, Sally Freeman. I saw you in the hotel in Oak Creek.'

'Thought so.'

'Did they tell you....?'

He knew what she was going to ask and cut in. 'Yes. Those men killed Consuela.'

'One of the boys made a coffin.'

'Yes.'

'Ralph Coates, isn't it?'

'Right.'

'You need a doctor.'

The sound that came out of his throat was like a despairing groan.

'There isn't one in Oak Creek?' Sally surmised from his reaction.

'No.'

'I don't know what's best for all those cuts.'

'Could one of....'

38

'Yes?'

'....the men ... ride to the hotel and tell Gilbert?'

'Will he know what to do? Does he have some medical knowledge?'

'Yes.'

Roy Durwood moved forward, seeing a way out of their predicament. 'I'll go,' he offered, eager to hand over responsibility for the mutilated man to someone who knew him.

Sally raised her eyes to meet his. 'You think that's wise, Roy? What happens if those men come back?'

'I'll leave Carl in charge. He'll know what to do.'

'Why don't you send Carl and you stay here?'

'Because the hotel man don't know Carl. He does know me.'

Coates could see the woman was not happy with Durwood's line of reasoning, but her silence indicated she could think of no further objections.

'You'd best eat before you leave,' she said with resignation.

Durwood was in the act of saddling his steeldust when he heard the sound of hoofbeats. He saw the trio halt as they became aware of the smoke rising from the chimney. Durwood crossed to the house and alerted the others.

'We've gotten company!' he announced.

Sally Freeman's heart thundered in her chest.

'Arnold and Brian have just gone out to dig the grave!'

'I'll get them,' Ranahan offered, and hurried out back.

By the time the three men returned to the house the trio of strangers had ridden closer, irked by what they saw. The strung-up, dead body they had expected to find was missing and the painted sign had been torn down.

'Looks like somebody found him, Lou,' Keith Tweedy announced needlessly.

'Ain't nothin' wrong with your eyes, Keith. Leave the talkin' t'me.'

They halted ten yards from the house and surveyed the four men standing staring at them, hands loosely on their hips, ready for any eventuality.

'Howdy,' Lou Pike offered in greeting, showing his teeth.

'Howdy yourself,' Roy Durwood responded. 'You looking for someone in particular?'

'Feller by the name o' Coates.'

'Now ain't that a coincidence? So are we. Arranged to meet him here. Found the place deserted, apart from a dead Mexican woman. You know anything about her?'

Now in full control of himself, Pike said, 'Dead, you say?'

'Dead. Shot three times. You figure Coates did

40

that?'

'Hell!' Pike snorted irritably. 'How would I know?'

'You know Coates well?'

'No. Heard he might be hirin'. Rode here to find out.'

None of them needed telling that was a blatant lie. What work could a homesteader offer three men?

Carl Ranahan got into the conversation. 'Looks like you had a wasted trip.'

'Looks that way.'

Pike scraped a hand across a three-day growth of bristles. 'You tell Coates we dropped by when he comes back, huh?'

'We'll do that,' Ranahan agreed. '*If* he comes back. You feel like informing the sheriff in Oak Creek about the dead woman?'

Pike swung his mount around as he said, 'You found her; you tell him.'

He rode off followed by his two pards. They didn't look back.

'You figure they're the ones who did it, Roy?' Arnold Glover queried.

'I'd lay odds on it. The question is, what will they do now? They sure as hell know we were lying through our teeth, just as we know they were.'

FIVE

'More to the point,' Ranahan said, 'is what do *we* do?'

'What d'you mean?'

'Too risky for you to ride into Oak Creek now. They could be lying in wait for you between here and town. We don't have to like it, but we thwarted their plan by saving that man from a terrible death.'

'I don't think he's out of the wood yet, Carl.'

Ranahan eyed Durwood objectively, reading his mind. 'You wish he had died, don't you? Him living messes up our plans.'

'Don't you reckon *he* wishes he was dead? All

43

that pain? If he does live, he'll never be the man he was.'

'If he survives, he'll be a one-man wave of vengeance. I'd hate to be those men if Coates recovers and sets out after them.'

Impressed by the deep baritone resonance in Ranahan's voice, Durwood agreed. 'Yeah. Could be you're right.'

'So what happens now?' They all turned at the sound of Sally Freeman's voice.

'I guess we'll have to discuss that, Sal,' Durwood replied. 'Carl thinks it would be too risky for me to go back to Oak Creek.'

'I heard. But won't it be just as risky to stay here?'

'My sentiments exactly.'

'We can't ride away and leave him, Roy. They'd come back and kill him for sure if we left.'

'You know we wouldn't do that, Sally,' Ranahan reassured her. 'When we go, we take him with us.'

'You think he's fit to travel?' she asked scornfully.

'There's a buckboard out there,' Carl said, nodding to his right. 'We could pack it with bedding and make him comfortable. There must be a doctor in El Paso, and he needs medical attention.'

Arnold Glover said, 'I guess the first thing to do is bury that woman. Come on, Brian, let's get to it.'

* * *

They told him what they had decided, and Ralph Coates could raise no flicker of objection. He was in too much pain to care what they did and he knew that as long as he stayed where he was there was the danger of his attackers returning, with reinforcements, to finish him off, and maybe his benefactors as well.

'It's not a bad road between here and El Paso,' Carl Ranahan assured him, forgetting that Coates probably knew the trail far better than he did. 'We'll make you as comfortable as we can. You survived that whipping, I guess you can cope with a thirty mile ride. Sally has done all she can for you. You need a doctor.'

Coates closed his eyes and left his fate in their hands.

'You did a good job of cleaning him up, young lady. This is the most barbarous attack I've ever seen on any man. I'll put some antiseptic salve on his wounds and then all we can do is let time be the healer, but I fear he is already in the throes of a fever. He'll need a lot of nursing.'

There was a questioning look in the doctor's glance. Sally knew he expected some sort of response.

'He's a stranger to us, Doctor.'

'Well he can stay here for a while, but I have a living to earn. I can't be doctor *and* nursemaid.'

'All right. I'll stay with him.'

Durwood protested. 'You know you can't do that, Sal.'

'It won't be for long, Roy. We can't abandon him. There's no one else. You go on with the others. I'll join you as soon as I can.'

Durwood sighed heavily, his frustration near to breaking point, but he did not want Sally to think he had no feelings towards the unfortunate Coates. 'I'll come back for you in a week,' he said. 'I don't want you riding to Las Cruces alone.'

She smiled her appreciation of his concern as he turned on his heels and went out into the street.

His three comrades gazed at him expectantly. 'Sally is gonna play nursemaid for a week. Let's put on a feedbag and then find ourselves a bed for the night. Tomorrow we head back to Las Cruces.'

The fever lasted five days, but when he came out of it the intensity of the pain created by the cuts in his flesh had eased. On the sixth morning he looked into Sally Freeman's dark brown, anxious eyes, and summoned a wan smile. 'You're still here.'

'I did promise you I wouldn't leave you.'

'What about the men?'

'They've gone. Roy is coming back for me two

days from now.'

'Your husband?'

'Yes.'

'Am I in his bad books?'

'Of course not. He knows you needed nursing.'

'Where are we?'

'In the doctor's house. I've been sleeping on that cot over there.'

He closed his eyes and let out a groan. 'Can I turn over? I feel as stiff as a barn door.'

'You can turn on your side, but not your back. You're healing nicely and you don't want to undo all the good these last few days have done.'

He eased his position. 'I'm hungry.'

'I'll get you some broth.'

Later, his hunger assuaged, his curiosity gave rein to his tongue. 'Who are you?'

'You know who I am. I'm Sally Freeman.'

'Where do you come from Sally Freeman?'

'Ohio. My folks were farmers.'

'So what were you doin' in Texas?'

'Waiting for Roy. He'd had some business to do farther south.'

Their eyes held for long moments, while he debated the wisdom of asking what kind of business Roy Durwood was in. Why did he need three other men along with him on his business travels?

'You an' Roy been married long?'

'Three years.'

'And the others?'

'Friends of ours.'

'You travel together a lot?'

'Quite a lot.' She flashed him her most innocent smile. 'And that's enough questions for one day, Mr Ralph Coates. I'm so glad you're feeling better.'

'So am I, Sally, and I do thank you.'

'Now you rest. I need some fresh air. If the doctor comes in, you tell him I've just gone for a stroll. I won't be long.'

Dr Travers appeared a few minutes later. 'So,' he began, smiling with satisfaction, 'you're back with us. That was quite a fever you had. How are you feeling?'

'Stiff.'

'Want to try sitting up?'

'I guess.'

'Just swing your feet to the floor then. Easy does it.'

As he obeyed, Coates winced as shafts of pain shot through his back, but he soon felt the benefit of being able to move again.

'Seems like you offended some of those Texans, Mr Coates.'

'Offended them?' He stared at the doctor, then pushed out a grin. 'Reckon it's lucky for me I didn't make 'em good an' mad.'

The doctor's expression was sobering. 'Vengeance can be a great temptation, Mr Coates, but if I were you I'd forget it and head back to Arizona as soon as you're well enough to ride.'

'How come you know so much about me, Doc?'

'I happen to know a man you worked for last year. You located his missing daughter.'

'Lester Gleave.'

'Yes. We're old friends. He happened to mention you the last time we met.'

Coates nodded. 'How is he?'

'You'll be pleased to know he took his wife to see Polly a month ago. He was delighted to find he had two grandsons.'

That surprised Coates, considering they had been fathered by a man Lester Gleave hated, but he said, 'I'm glad.'

But Coates was not happy to be reminded that he had not seen his own folks for a long time.

Feelings of guilt swept through him, but he thrust them aside as his mind rejected the doctor's advice. Time enough to heed that after he had found the man who had killed Consuela Martinez so mercilessly. Coates would not be able to live with himself until that man was dead.

SIX

He came stumbling back from the privy to find Sally Freeman had returned. Leaning his weight against the door post, he fashioned a weak smile that betrayed his vulnerability.

'Getting ambitious, aren't you?' she said, making no attempt to assist him back to the bed.

'My legs feel like willow branches.'

'You haven't been on your feet for almost a week and you've been a very sick man. You need a hand?'

'No.' His breathing was slightly laboured. 'I have to make an effort.'

Leaning his weight against the wall and using

the furniture to assist his return, he sat down heavily on the edge of the bed and winced as the arrows of discomfort plagued his torn flesh.

'Don't try to rush your recovery. Patience has its own reward.'

He showed his teeth again. 'A female philosopher as well as a nurse, huh.'

'It's just commonsense.'

She waited for him to recover from his exertions, admiring his courage and the constitution that had brought him through an ordeal that would have killed most men. Had it not been for her commitment to Roy Durwood, she knew she would have been strongly drawn to this man. Consuela Martinez had been a woman of some discernment.

'I think I'd best lie down again for a spell. I'm weaker than I expected to be.'

'A wise decision. Anything I can get you?'

'Some hot coffee?'

'Coming up.'

When she left the room he began to assemble his hopes and fears into some coherent order. Consuela was dead and decently buried, so the promise she had extracted from him to protect her was now at an end. His failure to fulfil that promise felt like a knife twisting in his gut. Avenging her murder would go some way towards appeasing the anger that was building up inside him.

Sally Freeman would be gone within a couple of

days, but before she departed he needed as much information about her, Roy Durwood and his cohorts, and the men who had mutilated him as he could draw from her. He needed to know what assets he had been left with.

'There you are, try that.'

He forced himself upright again and took the steaming mug from her short-fingered hands. The hot java lifted his spirits, making him feel physically more robust. Sally watched him like a mother hen with only one chick, her smile of encouragement well in evidence.

'What happened to my guns, Sally?'

'Under the bed. Your horses and two saddles are down at the livery stables.' She nodded in the direction of a corner of the room. 'Your clothes and some money we found in your pockets are all over there. There's your buckboard and bedding down at the livery, too. We brought all we thought you'd need once you were fit again.' She laughed softly. 'We still weren't sure you'd make it, even with the doctor's help.'

'I guess I owe you, Sally.'

'Not just me. Roy and the others, especially Carl.'

'Carl?'

'Carl Ranahan. He was the one who sided with me all the way. He was really incensed by what had happened. If I hadn't agreed to stay and

53

nurse you, I think Carl would have done.'

'Which one is Carl?'

'The old man, as we call him. He's in his forties now.'

'The one with the beard?'

'That's right.'

'I hope I get the chance to thank him.'

She shrugged noncommittally.

He finished the coffee as the silence piled up between them. He must not push her. Gentle probing would be the easiest way to extract the information he needed.

She took the mug from him as he held it towards her, then he slowly reclined on his right side and settled his gaze upon her. A very attractive young woman, around a hundred and ten pounds, he estimated, which meant for her five feet and a few inches, her bones were nicely covered, without her being fat. He admired the long chestnut hair falling to her shoulders, the ends curling outwards. She reminded him of his dead wife, although Kate had been even more beautiful.

'After three years, how come you and Roy have no children?'

'I'm happy to say it just never happened.'

'You don't hanker for motherhood?'

'No, Mr Coates, I don't. Once a woman becomes a mother she's too dependent on the whims of her lord and master, as the English would say.'

'I can see you're a young woman with a strong mind of her own.'

'My folks would have had me marry some farmer and settle down in Ohio to raise his kids. That was why I opted to run off with Roy. His way of life offered excitement and travel.'

His worst fears were beginning to take root. 'Travel and excitement, huh?'

'That's what I said.'

'Yes. You mentioned yesterday you travelled a lot. Must be an interesting line of business your husband is in, especially with friends along all the time.'

His curiosity warned her to be careful. 'Roy needs protection,' she said lamely.

'From whom?'

She shrugged. 'Other men.'

'Bandits, or county sheriffs?'

'Why, Mr Coates, whatever are you suggesting?'

'I'm suggesting that Roy and his friends are in the money business. I never did come across a businessman who needed three bodyguards.'

'Well you have now.' She stood up and flounced towards the door. 'Excuse me, I need to have a word with Doctor Travers.'

So he was right. A band of outlaws had saved his life. The irony of it would have struck him as amusing if it had not been for the fact that he had so often fought on the side of law and order.

*   *   *

Dr Travers assisted Sally to remove the cot from the room, while Ralph Coates looked on with more than idle interest. Was the girl now afraid to spend another night in the same room with him?

Around seven o'clock she brought him supper. He eyed the steak, potatoes and gravy with relish. His appetite was beginning to assert itself again.

She left him to eat, sitting on the edge of the bed. When she returned with coffee and to collect his empty plate she avoided his gaze.

'What are you afraid of, Sally?'

Her eyes lifted defiantly. 'Afraid?'

'You've moved the cot out.'

'You don't need me to watch over you through the night any more. You'll learn soon enough not to lie on your back.'

'You're not leaving yet, are you?'

'No. I told you. Day after tomorrow.'

'Well don't desert me. I need someone to talk with.'

'What about?'

'You … and those men who whipped me.'

'I don't know who they are.'

'But you saw them. They came back while you were at the house, didn't they? I may have been in a lot of pain, but it didn't make me deaf. I heard the men talkin'. And you.'

56

'I don't know anything. Drink your coffee.'

She turned and left the room, leaving him feeling he'd blown every chance of eliciting her help.

SEVEN

She tended to his needs, brought him food and coffee at the normal times of day, but the innocent smile was absent from her lips. He felt the need of her companionship in his weakened state, and so he refrained from questioning her about her life as an outlaw's woman. Although she wore a wedding ring, he suspected that no preacher had ever blessed her union with Roy Durwood. Run off with him, she had said, and that meant no parental consent, either.

'You think Roy will let me come with you when you go off tomorrow?'

'You're in no condition to travel yet. You're too

weak, and even a shirt on your back would drive you crazy. How do you expect to be able to ride?'

He knew she was right. His weakness irritated him, but he had enough acumen to know that her earlier words about patience had to be heeded. There was no sense in trying to hurry nature's healing process. He needed to be fit and strong before he climbed into a saddle again.

'Will you be travelling far, Sally?'

'I don't know what Roy's plans are.'

'Will you come back and see me?'

'What for? You don't need me any more. Doctor Travers has already said you can stay here as long as you need.' She relented long enough to flash him a smile. 'He's rather proud of having brought you through that fever.'

'With a lot of help from you,' he reminded her.

She shrugged away the compliment. 'There was no one else.'

'You're a fine young woman, Sally.'

She eyed him questioningly. 'Was Consuela a fine young woman?'

'She was. She married young and was widowed not long afterwards. I promised to watch out for her. I failed her.'

'You didn't know how some Texans feel about men who consort with Mexican women?'

'No, I didn't. We met in New Mexico, where that kind of feeling is not as strong.'

'I'm sorry. It's none of my business what went on between the two of you.'

'She wanted to marry me, but....'

She waited for him to go on, but his voice trailed into silence. 'But you didn't?'

'No.'

'Why not? Because she was Mexican?'

'That had nothing to do with it. I was married myself once. My wife died.' He eyed her through a long silence. 'You remind me of her.'

'I'm sorry.'

He got to his feet and began to pace slowly around the room in an effort to put a little strength back into his legs. Being reminded of Kate only focussed his mind on the bleak future that stretched before him. Once he had avenged the killing of Consuela, what was there to look forward to any more?

Sally broke the brief silence. 'Doctor Travers was telling me you come from Arizona.'

'That's right.'

'Will you go back there ... after....?'

'After I've killed those butchers, you mean?'

'Yes.'

Perhaps he should. For two years now he had been running away from his memories, but not only that, his obligations, too. He had left Kate's brother to run the ranch alone and not even informed his own folks of her death. Disliking the feelings of guilt that swept over him, he switched his mind to more pressing matters.

'D'you think Roy could spare Carl Ranahan for a few weeks?'

'What for?'

'He saw those men clearly. I was too busy trying to fight them off to get a good look at them. They attacked me when I was half asleep.'

'Carl is not a violent man, Mr Coates.'

He turned to face her. 'My name is Ralph. I'd be obliged if you'd use it.'

'Ralph.'

'You said Carl was incensed by what those men did. I just figured he might want to do something about it.'

Her shoulders lifted and fell again. 'He felt so strongly about what happened to you that he paid the livery man to look after your horses and tack for two weeks.'

'You didn't mention that.'

'I shouldn't have mentioned it now. He won't thank me for it.'

He moved back to sit on the edge of the bed. 'So what do you think? Would he help me?'

'You'll have to ask him ... and Roy.'

Three weeks later Carl Ranahan returned to the doctor's house. He looked at Coates speculatively. 'Back still hurt?'

'I can bear a shirt on it, but I need exercise.

Fancy playin' nursemaid for a while?'

'So long as you promise not to go looking for trouble until you're fit enough to handle it.'

'I'm not a fool, Carl.'

'There's still some doubt about that.'

Coates knew exactly what he meant, but he had no intention of discussing his relationship with Consuela. He respected Ranahan's line of thinking.

For the next week the two men walked the main thoroughfare of El Paso, morning and evening, then it was decided Coates was strong enough to mount his horse again. Riding soon wearied him, but with perseverance and a gradual lengthening of the time he spent in the saddle each day, he made good progress, getting stronger and more confident as the days slipped by. In between their walking and their riding, both men practised using their handguns out along the trail that led south. Coates in particular realised how stiff and slow his gun hand had become. He would need to regain his old prowess before he and Ranahan went looking for the killer of Consuela Martinez.

The two men talked a lot, learning about each other, but it was not until they had said farewell to Dr Travers and ridden south that Coates raised the question of the manner in which Ranahan made his living.

'What put you on the wrong side of the law, Carl?'

Ranahan's head swivelled sharply. 'Did you work that out for yourself or did you drag it out of Sally?'

'Didn't take much workin' out. Four men and a woman, always on the move. I ran through everything else I could think of, but nothin' added up to make any sense. You had to be a robber gang. Banks, is it?'

'Yeah. Sally gathers the information, Roy does the planning. The rest of us just follow orders. We've had a few close shaves, but so far it's worked well.'

'What about the killin'?'

'Never had to do any. Roy's too smart for that. We always hit the bank just before closing time, when there aren't many folks on the streets. We threaten, but we never kill.'

'There'll be a first time, when one of you makes a mistake.'

'I try not to think about that.'

Obviously he had taken the possibility into account more than once.

'Where are they now, the others?'

'I dunno.' He flashed Coates an even-toothed grin through the greying beard. 'Matter of fact, I jumped at the chance to break away for a spell when Roy told me you wanted me along.'

'Like I told you before, you don't have to get involved, once you've identified those men for me.'

Ranahan made no comment, and Coates knew that the abhorrence the outlaw felt at what the gang had discovered the day Consuela had been shot was still fresh in his mind. Carl Ranahan would not back off when things began to get ugly.

Coates was beginning to feel wearied by the ride back to the house he had shared for such a short time with Consuela. He would be glad to get out of the saddle and ease the stiffness in his back.

Ranahan noticed him stretch and flex his muscles. 'It'll be a while yet before you can cope with trouble, Ralph. Don't say I didn't warn you.'

'So you did, Carl.' The admission irked Coates. He was so impatient to find the men who had whipped him with such brutality that he almost wished he had an equally sadistic streak in his own make-up. It was small comfort to know that Consuela had not been ravished before they'd killed her.

Both men drew rein within sight of the old homestead, puzzled. Where the house and stables should be standing there was nothing to see.

They moved their horses forward at a walk, their eyes gradually telling them how wise Roy Durwood and Ranahan had been in opting to leave so suddenly for El Paso. Those men had returned, probably with others, to exact a price for the life of Ralph Coates. There was nothing but grey ashes and blackened, partially burnt timbers where the buildings had once stood in a flat expanse west of the mountains.

Ralph Coates became aware of a mounting fury rising within him. Had they known he was no longer there when they had torched the house?

He knew it wouldn't have made any difference. They were the sort of men who would have exulted in watching him burn alive.

EIGHT

Coates rode around the perimeter of the devastation, then his gaze fastened on a point where he himself had dug two graves the year before. Now there was a third and he steered his mount towards it. The mound of earth was still fresh, but drying into a cracked surface under the hot sun that poured constantly onto this area of Texas. The arsonists must have come at night, he decided, or they would surely have desecrated the three graves to complete their mission of hate.

He eased himself out of the saddle and bared his head. At a distance, Carl Ranahan watched him as Coates stood quite still by the side of

Consuela Martinez' grave, wondering if he was praying. After a while the tall, blond man pushed his hat back onto his head and remounted. He rejoined Ranahan.

'At least they let her rest in peace, Carl.'

'I guess we should be thankful for small mercies, but right now I'm feeling murderous.'

'That makes two of us.'

'What now?'

'The hotel in Oak Creek.'

'You sure you ain't too weary to ride that far?'

The rage burning within him outweighed his weariness. 'I can make it if you can.'

'You'd better pray there's a vacant room when we get there.'

Gilbert Perry welcomed the two men, showing no obvious surprise that Coates was accompanied by this stranger. He wondered what had happened to the Mexican woman and took the opportunity to make a polite inquiry.

'How is Mrs Martinez?'

'She's dead, Gilbert. Murdered by sadists.'

Shocked into a momentary silence, Perry stared open-mouthed for several seconds, then he said, 'I'm sorry to hear that, Ralph.'

But now he began to suspect why Sheriff Herb Adelman had been making inquiries about Ralph Coates recently.

'I'll tell you all about it in the mornin'. Right now I need a bed and some hot food. You can accommodate us?'

'You want separate rooms?'

'Not necessarily.'

'We've a room with two beds vacant. I'll just ask Liz to rustle up a meal for you, then I'll take you up.'

Coates retired early, reluctantly admitting the long ride had exhausted him. Carl Ranahan went in search of Gilbert Perry.

'Can you spare me a few minutes in private, Mr Perry?'

'Surely, Mr Ranahan.' He led the way to his private lounge and motioned Ranahan to take an armchair. 'What can I do for you?'

'My guess is that Ralph will only tell you half the story, so I figure you ought to know he was tied to a corral pole and severely whipped when those men killed Consuela Martinez. He's lucky to be alive. If I and some of my friends had not ridden by that same morning, he would have roasted to death under the hot sun.'

A deep frown corrugated Perry's brow. 'Who would do such a thing?'

'Texans who can't forget the Alamo. The kind who hate a white man with a Mexican woman. They nailed a board alongside him with the message "Mex lover" painted on it. A plain warning to others.'

'And the woman? Was she....?'

'Mercifully, no. They shot her three times. She must have died instantly.'

Ranahan waited while Perry absorbed the impact of what he was trying to convey.

'And now you and Ralph are planning to take revenge on those men?'

'Would you expect anything less? Evil men have no compassion; no mercy on anyone, man, woman, or child. If they're allowed to get away with it this time, how long before they do it again?'

In spite of his own activities as a bank robber, Ranahan did not number himself as one of the evil men.

'I abhor violence, Mr Ranahan, but in this instance I have every sympathy. I just hope Ralph will allow the law to punish those men and not try to do it himself.'

It was not an idea that had even crossed Ranahan's mind, but he refrained from commenting. Hanging, he figured, was too good for the men they were seeking.

'The thing is, Mr Perry, if I describe these men to you, can you put names to them?'

'I can try.'

'A short man who snarls rather than smiles. Not too particular about shaving. He had several days' growth on his face the day I saw him. Cold, cruel eyes.'

'Aaron Veldon employs a man who could fit that description, but I'd hate to....'

'Who is this Aaron Veldon?'

'Rancher. Has a large spread to the south. In his early sixties, grey hair and moustache. Always well groomed, but known to hate Mexicans.'

'Sounds promising, but there was no old man amongst the three who called at the homestead the day after Ralph was beaten.'

'Oh, Veldon wouldn't indulge in violent acts himself. That's what he employs men like Lou Pike for.'

'The little man?'

'Yes.'

'Lou Pike. I'll remember that name. Now about the others. One was tall and gangly. Big, strong man, with long hair, laughing eyes and a constant smile, like it was fixed on his face.'

'Keith Tweedy, a sidekick of Lou Pike's.'

'Ahuh. And the third one was another big, husky feller, clean shaven, dark brown hair.'

'If the other two were Pike and Tweedy, then that would be Fred Daly. The three of them are always together whenever they come to town. As a matter of fact they – and Aaron Veldon – were in town the day Ralph and his lady friend left here a few weeks ago.'

'You sure about that?'

'Quite sure. I noticed them staring at Ralph that morning as he and Consuela rode away. I was out front at the time.'

'Thanks, Mr Perry. I think you've fingered the culprits.' He stood up and said, 'I'll turn in now. See you in the morning.'

'Goodnight, Mr Ranahan. Sleep well.'

Ranahan didn't sleep well. His mind was too full of what Perry had told him. If – and there was still a faint possibility of doubt in his mind – the hotelier had identified the men he and Coates were seeking, then it should not take long to find them.

While Coates washed, Ranahan related what he had discovered.

'Thanks, Carl.' Coates dried himself with some care. 'You've saved us a lot of time.' He was also thankful to have been spared the discomfort of explaining to Gilbert Perry about his failure to protect Consuela.

'There's still a chance they are not the same men. We have to be sure before we act, but I'm fairly confident the names Perry gave me are the ones we're looking for.'

'At least it's a startin' point. How's my back lookin'?'

'Raw.' The scars were like thin ropes plastered

to the flesh, still red and repulsive. They zig-sagged all over his back in such profusion there was little unmarked flesh visible. 'Enough to put a man off his breakfast. The thing is, does it still pain you?'

'Not much, but I was glad to get my shirt off last night.'

'Well get it back on and let's go and eat.'

Still convinced that Coates was not yet fit enough for his mission of retribution, Ranahan counselled patience. 'I suggest we stay here in town and let them come to us. If we go out to Veldon's ranch we'll be on their home ground, giving them the advantage.'

'We could wait around for weeks,' Coates objected.

'My impression is that these men come to Oak Creek to let off steam fairly frequently. If I'm any judge of men, they don't cotton to riding fence all that much. That's not what Veldon employs them for. They're his hard men.'

'Did you manage to find out why he needs hard men around him?'

'No, I didn't, but I guess rustlers operate down there, same as other places.'

They were back in their room after breakfast, and now Coates strapped his gunbelt around his hips. He shucked the shells out of the chamber and tossed them on the bed. Then he dropped the empty Colt .44 back into the holster and for five minutes he practised lifting it and taking aim at Ranahan from different angles.

'I thought Roy was fast on the draw,' Ranahan commented, 'but he'd never live with you.'

'I think I'm nearly back to my best. All that practice these past two weeks has paid off.'

'You think it's gonna be important?'

'Never can tell, but if this Lou Pike is Veldon's gunny, then it could be crucial.'

He replaced the shells in the chamber and dropped the gun back into leather. 'You still think we should report Consuela's murder to the sheriff?'

'Can you think of a good reason why not?'

'Don't see he can do much about it if we do. It's beyond his bailiwick. And it happened six weeks ago. My impression of Herb Adelman is that he is content to sit on his ass and draw his pay check once a month. Not a man to go lookin' for trouble.'

'You're acquainted?'

'We've met.'

A silence stretched between them as Ranahan ruminated. His own inclination was to steer clear of all lawmen, but he knew Gilbert Perry would expect Coates to report the murder. If he failed to do so, Perry would wonder why.

'Can't hurt to talk to the law, can it?'

Coates eyed him in surprise. 'You prepared to come with me?'

'You don't need me along. Besides, he knows you.'

'And you'd rather he didn't get to know you?'

A hard glint flashed in Ranahan's blue-grey eyes. 'I agreed to finger these men for you. I don't have to get involved with no sheriff!'

And we both know why, Coates mused, but he thought better of voicing it out loud.

'Suppose you get the horses while I slip in to see Adelman?'

'I'll do that. You need a ride to take the stiffness out of your back after yesterday.'

But when they descended the stairs together they saw the sheriff in conversation with Gilbert Perry.

It would have looked suspicious if they had turned back, so Coates fashioned a smile and said, 'Mornin', Sheriff.'

Ranahan continued to the street, saying nothing.

Ignoring the pleasantries, Adelman barked, 'How come you never reported the killing of this Mexican woman, Mr Coates?'

NINE

'I was just on my way to do that,' Coates answered, his smile vanishing, irritated by the harsh note in the sheriff's voice, 'but what you can do about it I cain't imagine. That homestead is out o' your territory.'

Adelman did not take kindly to being reminded of his limited authority. 'Let's take a walk down to my office, then we can make your report official.'

Coates slung a questioning look at Gilbert Perry.

'*I* didn't tell him, Ralph. He already knew.'

The sheriff motioned Coates to lead the way, then fell into step beside him once they were out on the street. They made the short walk without saying a word.

Seated behind his desk, Adelman indicated that Coates should take the chair opposite. 'That place may be out of my jurisdiction, Coates, but I've received a report that the old Wallace place has been burnt out and there's a new grave out there. Would that be the resting place of this Mexican friend of yours?'

'That's right.'

'You buried her?'

'No. I was roped to the corral when she was shot and in no condition to do anything about it afterwards. Some friends o' mine buried her.'

'Can you prove any of this?'

'Do I have to?'

'I reckon so. The report I had was that you had killed her yourself, then set fire to the place and vanished.'

Coates frowned. 'Who made that report?'

'The most prominent man in these parts, so I have to take it seriously. Unless you can prove you didn't do it, I'll have to detain you pending the county sheriff's investigation.'

Coates stood up, unbuckled his gunbelt and laid it on the chair, then stripped off his shirt and turned his back on the sheriff. 'That proof enough for you?'

Adelman gasped when he saw the ugly scars

covering the younger man's back. 'Hell and damnation! Who did that t'you?'

Putting his shirt back on, Coates said, 'That's what I'd like to find out. I was attacked by three men early in the mornin' when I was half asleep. By the time I came to after one of them knocked me cold I was roped to that corral and my back was bared for the whippin'. I heard Consuela cry out, then three shots. I guessed she was dead.'

'And you've no idea who these men were?'

'Oh, yes, I've a very good idea. I've also a very good idea who your prominent man is who made that report. Aaron Veldon?'

Momentarily silenced by the accuracy of Coates' query, the sheriff blurted, 'He was only doing his civic duty.'

'How did he know about the fire?'

'One of his men reported it, so Aaron rode out to see for himself. He figured you'd had a spat with the woman, then gotten rid of her after you found out how Texas folk feel about a man bedding a Mexican woman.'

Coates was strapping on his gunbelt again. 'You've no proof I was bedding her, Sheriff!'

'It's what everybody around here was thinking.'

'Well they were wrong!'

'You'll have a hard time convincing folks.'

It was a point Coates was obliged to concede, although he did not admit it to Adelman.

He rested his hands on the desk and stared hard at the sheriff. 'Just when did Veldon make this accusation?'

'A month ago, maybe longer. It wasn't until this morning I heard you were back in town.'

'Well you should know enough about me by now to dismiss any idea o' me killin' a woman.'

Steepled hands touched his chin as Adelman considered his response. 'I did find it hard to believe, which was why I didn't arrest you right there in the hotel lobby, but when a man of Veldon's standing comes to me with that kind of information, I'm obliged to sit up and take notice.'

'And did he tell you which of his men reported the fire to him?'

'Matter of fact he did. Feller by the name of Lou Pike.'

'You've just convinced me it *was* Lou Pike who shot Consuela, an' two more o' Veldon's men who whipped me that mornin'. Now why don't you go out and arrest them?'

A muscle jumped where Adelman's cheek and jawbone met. His mouth went dry and he stared back at Coates in silence.

'Well?'

The sheriff lowered his gaze, dropped his hands on the desk and stared at them. Coates knew without being told that the man didn't have the guts to even make a token attempt at the arrest.

The streak of fear in his make-up was almost visible.

'I need proof, Coates.' His eyes lifted defiantly. 'You don't have any.'

'You've seen my back. You've been told about the shootin'. What more do you want?'

'I believe what you've told me, but you've no proof it was Veldon's men who did it.'

'So you intend to do nothin'?'

'There's nothing I *can* do.'

'But you were plannin' on arrestin' me on the sayso of a man who wasn't even there!'

The silence lasted a long time.

Coates turned and went to the door. Adelman watched him go with a sinking feeling in his guts. Intuition told him that Lou Pike's days were numbered.

His balled fists relaxed into fingers and thumbs again as Coates hit the street and saw Carl Ranahan astride his roan, the reins of Coates' mount held lightly alongside. Without a word Coates climbed into the saddle and led the way out of town on the south trail. Ranahan respected his thoughtful silence until he could contain his interest no longer.

'Ain't you gonna tell me what happened?'

Coates gave him a summary of his conversation with Adelman, then concluded, 'I reckon we don't need any more proof about the identity of the men we're lookin' for. Why would Aaron Veldon take the trouble to ride out to look at the damage the fire had done if he didn't have a personal interest? How come it was Lou Pike who reported the facts to him?'

'Because it was Lou Pike and his pards who were responsible.'

'Exactly. The question is, did they do it under orders from Veldon or was it Pike's own idea?'

'We could ask him,' Ranahan said facetiously.

Coates slanted a glance at him that Ranahan ignored, his gaze concentrated on the trail ahead.

'I still think, Ralph, we should be patient and wait for the right opportunity to get Pike and his two pards away from the ranch. Getting ourselves killed on their territory, where the odds stack up against us, would defeat the whole objective.'

Coates knew he was right. He also recognized that he was still not as fit as he would like to be and a day or two more to gather his strength and harden his mutilated back would be a wise move. It was a luxury he was destined to be denied.

The furnace heat of the sun began to feel like the wrath of God on his back as they wheeled their horses for the return to Oak Creek, and he was glad to reach the shelter of the livery stables. He unsaddled his mount and gave him a rub down.

They were in time for lunch at the hotel and both men ate with relish. The remainder of the day stretched before them like a burden. Eager to get on with their mission, prudence decreed a waiting game.

Ranahan suggested a little poker in the Mulehead Saloon, but Coates had never been a gambler and rejected the suggestion. 'You go ahead if you feel like it, Carl.'

'What will you do?'

'I'll have a chat with Gil and see what I can find out about those men that might be useful.'

'I might learn a thing or two in the saloon, without asking any direct questions,' Ranahan said.

'Be careful. You're all the help I've gotten.'

The Mulehead Saloon was alive with activity when Coates and Ranahan pushed through the door towards eight o'clock that evening. The ladies of the night wore their smiles with practised seductiveness and one of them left her study of the blackjack game and sidled up to Coates as the two men reached the bar.

'Why, Mr Coates. I'd heard you'd gone back to Arizona.'

There was no welcoming smile as he faced her. 'Who told you that?'

She shrugged. 'It's common knowledge, only it

must have been just a rumour.'

'As you can see for yourself.'

'Is it also a rumour about the homestead bein' burnt out?'

'Where did you hear that?'

'Keith Tweedy told me. Is it true?'

'It's true all right.'

She smiled ingratiatingly. 'And what happened to your lady friend? She gone back to New Mexico?'

'Didn't your friend Tweedy tell you?' Coates countered.

'Tell me what?'

'Consuela was murdered.'

'Murdered! Who by?'

'A feller by the name of Lou Pike. You know him?'

Her shoulders shuddered. 'Oh yes, I know him all right. He's capable of anything.'

'So you're not surprised?'

'Shocked, more than anything. When did it happen?'

'Six weeks ago. You seen this Lou Pike lately?'

Her eyes looked past him in the direction of the door. 'Don't look now, but he's just come in.'

Carl Ranahan lowered his beer glass to the mahogany as he heard the quiet warning. He eased casually to his left before turning around, his right hand on his gunbutt. As he faced the door he saw that Keith Tweedy stood on Pike's right, gazing around the room, while Fred Daly was moving forward.

'Move!' Ralph Coates said to the woman and she obeyed with some alacrity.

It was her sudden movement that grabbed Lou Pike's attention. In the instant he spotted Coates by the bar his hand flew to his gun and Coates flung himself sideways, cannoning into a man who was moving towards the bar. Coates lost his balance as he drew his Colt.44 and the room exploded in a cacophony of gunfire.

TEN

Lou Pike's first shot thudded into the woodwork of the bar, but his second hit the man who had caused Ralph Coates to lose his balance as the two men fell in a heap, with Coates underneath. The jarring of his tender back muscles made him wince, but fortunately his right hand, holding his Colt .44 was free and he fired back at Lou Pike. The little gunman spun round as the bullet thumped into his left shoulder. He turned and fled out into the street as Coates loosed off another shot, missing the target.

Coates pushed the wounded stranger off and scrambled to his feet, to discover that Fred Daly had been much too slow in palming his own gun. He was doubling over, gut-shot by Carl Ranahan.

The long-haired Keith Tweedy was not packing a gun but he was hurtling headlong towards Coates, his huge fists bunched, ready to strike. Never one to shoot an unarmed man, Coates swayed away from the punch aimed at his jaw and hit the big man over the head with his Colt. Tweedy collapsed on top of the wounded man who had gotten in the way of Lou Pike's bullet.

A quick glance towards the door and Coates observed that Fred Daly was not quite done with, his gun now aimed at Carl Ranahan again. Ranahan shot him through the heart.

When the gunfire ceased there was an eerie silence for all of three seconds, then the men and women who had scattered to the corners of the bar room all began babbling at once. Coates moved up alongside Ranahan.

'He's dead, Ralph.'

'Let's get after Pike!'

'Careful!' Ranahan counselled. 'He could be waiting for you to go out there.'

'I doubt it. He'll be hightailin' it back to the ranch if I'm any judge. We need to stop him.'

But as Coates went through the door, followed by Ranahan, he knew he was too late. Pike was already mounted and heading south out of town, too far away to make a shot worthwhile.

88

'There's a wounded man back in there. We'd best take a look at him, Carl.'

Ranahan followed Coates back inside. The man was sitting up, grimacing with pain, propped against the bar, surrounded by onlookers, none of whom seemed to be doing anything to help. Coates barged his way through and knelt beside the man. 'I'm sorry, mister. That bullet was meant for me.'

'It hurts like hell,' he croaked through tight lips.

Coates looked up. 'Carl. Go get Gilbert Perry.'

He turned back to the man as Ranahan moved away. 'There's no doctor here in town, but a friend o' mine might be able to help. I'm real sorry you had to walk in just when you did.'

'Who are you? Why was somebody ... tryin' t'kill you?'

'It's a long story. Tell you later.'

'Carry him into the back room,' a voice entreated. 'He'll be more comfortable there.'

Coates stood up. 'Who are you?'

'Jed Stokes. I own this place.'

There was no shortage of hands willing to pick the man up and carry him away from the gawping crowd that surrounded him. Stokes directed them to lay him on the couch as he cried out in agony.

'What's your name, mister?' Coates queried.

Jed Stokes answered for him. 'Joe Landis. He's the watchmaker.'

It was several minutes more before Gilbert Perry arrived with his bag of first aid equipment. Coates helped him to remove the man's coat and shirt, while Ranahan supported him. Then they laid him on his belly. Perry swabbed away the blood with a clean piece of linen, then sighed heavily as he saw how deeply the bullet was buried in the man's back.

He looked at Landis candidly. 'There's no easy way to tell you this, Joe, but if I try to get that bullet out I could kill you.'

'And if you don't?'

Perry shrugged. 'You could make it. Men have carried bullets around in them for years.'

'But I could die?'

'I can try to stop the bleeding. If I make an attempt to remove the bullet I'm sure to damage your back muscles and it will hurt like hell. I've no ether to give you.'

'Can't you knock me out somehow?'

'We could fill you full of whiskey to deaden the feeling, but it will still hurt.'

'It hurts now. Have a go, Gil. It can't be any worse than it is already.'

'You're wrong about that, but if you're sure that's what you want....?'

They forced whiskey into him and Perry used more to sterilize the wound, then set to work with a two-pronged instrument the like of which

Coates had never seen before. Luckily for him, the pain swamped Joe Landis and he fainted.

Seeing the man was beyond all feeling for at least a little while, Perry abandoned excessive care and dug deeply. The bullet came part way out, then the prongs slid off and blood poured out, obstructing Perry's view of the slug. He dug blindly until he got another grip and eased the lead free.

He worked frantically to stem the blood flow but it seemed like a hopeless task. 'Get me more cloths, Jed!'

By the time the wound was plugged, Joe Landis was conscious again but badly weakened.

'He must not be moved before morning, Jed. If he starts bleeding again he'll die. He's already lost far too much. Is there anyone who can stay and watch over him through the night?'

'I'll do that,' Coates offered.

Ranahan protested. 'But what about Lou Pike, Ralph?'

'He can wait, Carl. We know where to find him, and remember he's got a bullet in him as well. Go find Adelman and report what's happened. Get him to lock up that long-haired feller.'

'I heard somebody say the sheriff left town this morning. Nobody's seen him since.'

'Now I wonder where he went?'

But Coates already had an idea.

Ranahan said, 'We'd best hawgtie that big feller and see if we can lock him up somewhere.'

'Let's do that before he begins to get his senses back.'

Moments later they saw that fate had played the hand against them. Keith Tweedy was nowhere to be seen.

'What happened to Tweedy?' Coates asked the apron.

'You've only just missed him. He went out about a minute ago.'

'Why the hell didn't you stop him?' Ranahan demanded of the men standing around exercising their vocal chords in conjecture about what had happened earlier.

'Because when Tweedy hits a man he stays hit. None of us want fractured ribs or a broken jaw,' one of the men answered with some forcefulness.

The glint of fury in Ranahan's eyes was plain to see and the men looked away from it. Ralph Coates attempted to calm him.

'Go back to the hotel, Carl, and get some sleep. There's nothin' we can do about it tonight.'

'I'm not sleepy. You go and get some rest. I'll sit with the watchmaker for a spell.'

Coates could see the anger was still churning inside Ranahan, so he agreed, planning to relieve him later in the night.

'In that case, I'll do as you suggest. I'll be back

to relieve you around two o'clock.'

The undertaker arrived with a pine box to collect the dead Fred Daly, a scene watched by ghoulish eyes. He looked at a man with whom he was obviously well acquainted. 'Give me a hand, Bert?'

Bert duly obliged.

It was still early and Coates was not sleepy, either. Gilbert Perry emerged from the rear, his instructions to Jed Stokes concerning Joe Landis made clear, and Coates sidled alongside him as the hotelier left the saloon.

'Changed your mind about watching over the wounded man?'

'Carl wanted to take first watch. I'll go back later.'

It was a short walk to the hotel and a surprise awaited them both. Perry's face broke into a smile of welcome as he saw Roy Durwood and Sally Freeman in consultation with Liz Perry. All three of them turned as the two men entered.

'Why, Mr Freeman!' Perry greeted. 'Nice to see you again.'

'And you, Mr Perry. Your wife tells me we're in luck. That room we had last time is free.'

'Only just. It was vacated this morning.'

Coates stood and watched the exchanges, questions prowling around in his head. What were they doing here? What had motivated this sudden return to Oak Creek? Was Roy Durwood planning another bank raid in Texas so soon after the last one? Had they come to reclaim Carl Ranahan for the purpose?

Sally Freeman's gaze was fixed on him through the moments of conjecture. 'Hello, Ralph. How are you?'

'I'm doin' fine, Sally. How about you?'

'Just fine. Where's Carl?'

'He's keepin' watch over a wounded man right now.'

'Anyone we know?'

'No. Local watchmaker. He took a bullet intended for me.'

The news concentrated the minds of the newcomers with such eagerness to learn more that only Liz Perry's voice broke the silent, charged atmosphere.

'Is there anything I can get for you, Mrs Freeman, or do you want to go straight up to your room?'

ELEVEN

Explanations came as Roy Durwood and Sally Freeman waited for the cold, late supper that Liz Perry was preparing for them.

'We got worried about the two of you trying to run those men down,' Sally said.

Coates figured they were more concerned about Carl Ranahan than him. What were their intentions? He asked them.

Durwood remained silent, but after a brief hesitation, Sally answered, 'We know how Carl feels about those men, but he's not known for his prowess with a gun. We decided the two of you might need a little help.'

'Accordin' to what Carl has told me, none of you are experienced when it comes to gunfights, and that is what this situation is developin' into. Carl has already killed one of the men we're after. In fact he's no fool with a gun.'

He waited for that snippet of information to settle in their minds as they exchanged glances, worry settling in their eyes as they looked back at him.

'What exactly happened?' Durwood asked.

Coates told them.

'So this Lou Pike is already wounded?'

'But not seriously. He had enough savvy and strength to mount his horse and ride off into the night. We figure he'll head back to the ranch where he's employed. Seems likely the long-haired feller will do likewise.'

'So what do you aim to do now?'

'We've laid no plans. Could depend on you.'

Durwood's gaze was cautious. 'Meaning?'

'Have you simply come down here to get Carl back, or do you really mean you've come to help get those skunks?'

'Is Carl in the clear as far as the law is concerned?'

'The law in this town is a joke. My guess is that Sheriff Adelman does whatever Aaron Veldon tells him t'do, but I cain't prove that. Strikes me as mighty strange that Adelman is missin' just when he's needed. How come Lou Pike an' his pards show up in town when the sheriff is absent?'

'You mean the sheriff rode out to Veldon's ranch to tell him you were back here in Oak Creek?' Durwood suggested.

'Too much of a coincidence, don't you think?'

'Sure looks that way.'

'Be interestin' t'see if Adelman is back in the mornin'.'

'Yeah.'

Discussion ceased as Liz Perry came in with cold meat and bread for the new arrivals. 'Coffee coming right up,' she informed them, disappearing again.

Coates got to his feet. 'I'll say goodnight and leave you to your supper.'

Lou Pike knew he would never understand how he had managed to climb into his saddle after his escape from the saloon. The agonising pain in his shoulder got worse instead of better as he rode into the night, intent on getting back to the Veldon ranch as quickly as possible. His shoulder bone seemed to be broken but he didn't think the bullet had lodged there. Veldon would patch him up, he reasoned, whatever the injury might be. The rancher had been a major in the Confederate Army during the Civil War and was no stranger to the sight of gunshot wounds.

Three miles out of town his mount began to slow, blowing hard, and Pike allowed the buckskin to reduce his pace to a walk. Waves of nausea ebbed and flowed as he tried to listen for the sounds of pursuit. Relieved by the absence of hoofbeats, he wondered what had happened to Fred Daly and Keith Tweedy. He feared the worst, otherwise they would have followed him. He had caught a glimpse of the bearded feller firing at Fred as the bullet from Coates' gun spun him around, facing the door, and instinct had told him to get the hell out of the place before Coates fired again and killed him. It was damn bad luck that his aim at Coates had been thwarted by the watchmaker stepping in front of him at the crucial moment. Joe Landis had taken the bullet as he fell on top of Coates. The silly old fool was probably dead. Damn the man. If he hadn't gotten in the way Coates would be dead and he, Lou Pike, would not have this terrible pain in his shoulder. His left arm hung down by his side, numbed and completely useless.

Wearied by the incessant pain, he passed by the bunkhouse and rode straight up to the main house and called out, 'Veldon!'

The rancher was agonisingly slow to respond to the call and Pike yelled at the top of his voice, 'Veldon!'

Eventually Veldon came out onto the porch and

stared at him, slumped forward in the saddle. 'What in hell is wrong with you, Pike?'

'I've been shot. Shoulder.'

Sheriff Herb Adelman, who had followed Veldon to the door, stepped forward and hurried to Pike's side.

'Let's get you into the house, Lou.'

Pike almost fell into the sheriff's arms, and was then supported into the house.

'What happened, Lou?'

'That damned watchmaker got in front o' Coates just as I fired, then knocked him over. I missed with my second shot.'

The news sent the lawman into a blue funk. 'You mean Coates is still alive?'

'Yeah, but I'll get him next time. He was just lucky t'night.'

Ignoring Pike's spirited resolve, Aaron Veldon snapped, 'You shouldn't have come back here! Who do you think's gonna fix that shoulder for you here? You should've headed for El Paso and that doctor they've gotten there.'

'That's a fifty mile ride, boss!' Pike protested.

'It's another twelve miles from here, you fool!'

Dismay registered on Pike's face. 'You mean you ain't gonna fix me up?'

'Bullet still in there?' the rancher growled.

'No. It busted my shoulder bone an' it hurts like hell. We wuz only obeyin' your orders!'

'I pay you to troubleshoot, not get yourself shot up. You were supposed to get rid of this Coates feller, not let him get the better of you!'

Pike, in spite of his pain, shot back, 'I told you, that fool watchmaker walked in front of him just as I fired!'

'Dead?'

Pike blazed back, 'How the hell do I know? I didn't wait t'find out.'

Veldon, taking a grip on his anger at the failure of Pike's mission, pushed out a long, exasperated sigh. 'Let's take a look at you.'

'I'd best be getting back to town,' the sheriff said with some agitation.

'You do that, Herb. Find out what you can and see if you can't find some way of locking up that Coates feller. What I want to know is where have Fred and Keith gotten?'

'They could be dead, boss,' Pike said dispassionately. 'That Coates had a sidekick with him.'

'Who was he?'

'Dunno. Big feller, greying beard. His shooter was spittin' lead as I came out o' the Mulehead.'

Veldon turned to the sheriff. 'Looks like you might be able to arrest him for murder if Fred or Keith got themselves killed. You know Keith seldom packs a gun. Shooting an unarmed man is murder.'

'I'll look into it, Mr Veldon.'

Adelman turned and headed for the door, too squeamish to look at Pike's wound as Veldon helped the wounded man to get out of his coat. They heard the door close and his retreating footsteps as the sheriff went to collect his horse.

'He won't do nothin', boss. He's too lily-livered to try an' arrest either o' them fellers.'

'At least he's gotten enough sense to keep out of the way of bullets,' Veldon snapped back scornfully.

Gilbert Perry was relieved to find Joe Landis had survived the night without losing any more blood. The man was in considerable discomfort but nevertheless he expressed the wish to get back to his own modest dwelling, which combined shop and living quarters.

'Forget about work, Joe,' Perry advised. 'You need to rest completely until that wound starts to heal. You're weak from loss of blood and you need time to regain your strength. I'll find some woman to come and look after your needs. Cook for you and such.'

'My neighbour's wife already does that, Gil.'

'But can she spare the time to give you more attention?'

'Get me back to my place and you can ask her,' Landis said weakly, already feeling faint again.

Perry faced Jed Stokes, standing by listening to

the exchanges. 'Give me a hand to get him home, Jed?'

'Sure. But he don't look so good to me.'

Back at the hotel there was a conference in progress in Roy Durwood's room between him, Sally, Carl Ranahan, and Ralph Coates. After a while Ranahan said, 'I've been urging Ralph not to risk riding out to the Veldon ranch, but now there's five of us, maybe it's time we got this thing done with.'

'Six, Carl. You're not leaving me out of this.'

The men all stared at Sally Freeman, questioning her sanity.

Durwood warned, 'It could get very ugly out there, Sally.'

She smiled ingratiatingly. 'But I'll have you three, as well as Brian and Arnold to protect me. Besides, I want to see what men look like who would do what they did to Ralph.'

They took a vote on Ranahan's suggestion and agreed without question, although Durwood was reluctant to take Sally along.

'I still think you should stay here, Sal.'

'I'm coming, Roy. I can use a gun as well as any of you.'

Ralph Coates doubted that, especially as far as he himself was concerned. The young woman might be good at target practice, but shooting at a man who was shooting back was a different situation, especially when you had no experience of such danger.

'Let's go collect Brian and Arnold then,' Durwood said with a sigh of resignation.

The other two members of the Durwood gang had spent the night at the rooming house owned by Irishman Donal Kelly. Kelly, Quarmby and Glover had learned of the trouble in the Mulehead Saloon from another visitor.

'We heard about your trouble last night, Carl,' Quarmby said in greeting.

Ranahan glared back at him angrily. 'Then why didn't you come looking?'

'We knew you were all right and we didn't want to show our hand. Figured Roy wouldn't like it.'

His gaze switched to Roy Durwood as he said it.

'Too right I wouldn't. Let's ride. The sooner we're through with this business and back across the border the better I'll like it.'

'Just a minute there, you fellers!'

They all turned to face Sheriff Herb Adelman, hand on his gunbutt, his stance awkward in spite of his command.

Coates had seen the lawman ambling towards them and guessed he was nervous about challenging the group.

'Some other time, Sheriff,' he said. 'Right now we've gotten some urgent business with a killer.'

'Apprehending killers is *my* job, Coates, and you know it.'

'I also know you don't do a damn thing about it. I told you yesterday to arrest Lou Pike, but no, you ignored me. In case you're interested, he shot the town watchmaker last night.'

'I know that. I've just seen Jed Stokes. I've also been told one of your friends killed Fred Daly. I figured on talking to him about that.'

Ranahan defended himself. 'Self-defence, Sheriff. Anybody who was in the saloon last night would verify the fact.'

'I'd still like to talk to you in my office, mister.'

Taking his lead from the attitude Coates had adopted, Ranahan responded, 'Some other time, maybe. Like Mr Coates just explained, we've gotten a killer to apprehend.'

Ranahan turned his mount to face south and the others followed him, leaving the sheriff trembling with the agony of knowing he hadn't the guts to impose his authority on them.

Lou Pike roused himself from his bunk, adjusted the sling Aaron Veldon had fixed to hold his left arm steady and relieve the pressure on his shoulder, then looked at Keith Tweedy and said, 'How about that Veldon, Keith? Looks like he ain't gonna back us up when the showdown comes.'

'It was him told us to go lookin' for that Coates

feller, Lou.'

'Yeah. Now he wants t'be rid of us.' Pike grimaced as pain shot through him again. 'He told me I shoulda rode to El Paso to get the doc there to fix this shoulder.'

Tweedy ran fingers through his long hair. 'You told me last night, Lou.'

'I did?'

'Yeah.' Tweedy stretched and yawned. 'So what do we do, Lou?'

'I've been thinkin', mebbe we should quit an' ride to El Paso. I could see that doc there an' get some proper attention to this shoulder. Veldon never batted an eye when you came back last night an' told him Fred was dead. He didn't give a damn.'

'We'd have to avoid the town, Lou. We don't want to run into that Coates feller before you're fit to take him on again. You know I'm no good with a gun.'

'You have got one, Keith. Time to get some practice with it.'

'I'm better with my fists than a gun, Lou.'

'I know that, Keith, but there ain't no reason why you can't be good with both. All you need is some expert tuition.'

Tweedy smiled broadly, the eager light of anticipation in his brown eyes. 'You'll teach me, Lou?'

'Well it's a twenty dollar bill to a red cent nobody else will.'

His stomach rumbling, Tweedy's mind switched to a more immediate concern. 'I'm hungry, Lou. You comin' to eat? The other fellers went ten minutes since.'

'Sure. May as well get a bellyful o' Veldon's chow afore we ride off.'

Pike had no doubts that Keith Tweedy would still follow him. The big man alongside him would be a source of comfort in a situation he had never envisaged happening. No man wanted to be friendless when he was wounded.

TWELVE

'Some place!' Durwood exclaimed as they approached the Veldon ranch.

Long and sprawling, Spanish style, built of adobe, with a four feet high wall running round the main house, twin low gates giving access to the front of the casa. The gates were closed but their approach had apparently not gone unnoticed. An elderly man with white, well trimmed moustache was walking from the casa towards the gates, a black broad-brimmed hat shielding his head from the sun. He stood and waited for them. They drew up in a line, facing him.

'Howdy,' Coates said politely.

The greeting was not returned. 'You're Coates.'

'How did you guess?'

'No guess. I saw you in town one day.'

'You must be Aaron Veldon.'

'I am, and you're trespassing. What do you want?'

'Came to tell you one of your men got shot last night.'

Neat eyebrows lifted. 'Which one?'

'Feller by the name of Fred Daly.'

Veldon pretended he was unaware of the fact. 'Dead?'

Coates guessed Veldon was not all that surprised. Maybe somebody else had already told him. 'Afraid so. He tried to shoot one of us. We don't take kindly to that sort o' thing.'

'You making me responsible for that?'

'He worked for you. So does Lou Pike. You hidin' him?'

'Lou never hid from anybody in his life.'

'Mebbe he was never wounded before.'

'How did you know he was wounded?'

The man was becoming irritating with his evasive comments and questions. 'Because I'm the one who shot him!'

'Too bad, Coates. Lou is not likely to forget that. I'd watch out if I were you.'

Ranahan butted in. 'He's the one who needs to watch out. Where is he?'

'You've missed him. He left an hour or more since.'

'You expect us to believe that?'

Veldon's narrow-eyed gaze fastened on Ranahan. 'Mister, it makes no difference whether you believe it or not, it won't change anything.'

'Mind if I check your bunkhouse?'

'Yes, I do mind. I've already told you, you're trespassing.'

'I'll do it anyway.' Ranahan wheeled his horse. 'Brian, come with me, just in case Mr Veldon has a surprise waiting for us back there.'

Quarmby followed Ranahan and the two men disappeared around the back of the casa.

Veldon cast his eyes over the others, allowing them to dwell on Sally Freeman with appraisal.

'You like what you see, Mr Veldon?' she asked with bite in her voice.

'You're a fine looking young woman. What are you doing with these ruffians?'

'One of them is my husband. The others are my friends. We want Lou Pike and Keith Tweedy. Where are they?'

'I told you, Lou left, and Tweedy went with him.'

'Deserted you, did they?'

'I fired them, if you must know.'

'Because they failed to kill Mr Coates last night? That was the second failure, wasn't it? They tried to burn him alive in that old

109

homestead six or seven weeks ago.'

Roy Durwood cut in. 'Take it easy, Sal.'

She ignored him, her gaze fixed on Veldon as the rancher said, 'You're crazy, young lady. Lou would never do a thing like that.'

Ralph Coates said, 'Then why did you fire him?'

'That's my business.'

'We're makin' it ours.'

Sally said, 'You hate Mexicans, Mr Veldon. That is common knowledge. It was Lou Pike who killed Consuela Martinez and it was Keith Tweedy and Fred Daly who horsewhipped Ralph back at that homestead, and it was done on your orders.'

'I don't know what you're talking about, young woman, and now this conversation is at an end. Take your husband and your friends and get off my property.'

Something in his eyes as he stared insolently at her made Sally's skin crawl. Veldon was a man without human emotion, with the possible exception of hate. He would never admit it, but she was certain in her own mind that Ralph Coates had been brutalized and the Mexican woman killed on Aaron Veldon's orders. Any man who surrounded himself with killers of the calibre of Lou Pike was not fit to live. Suddenly consumed with hate herself, she drew her pistol from its holster and shot Veldon straight between the eyes.

The horses shuffled in alarm and their nostrils

flared at the smell of cordite, while their riders all stared at Sally Freeman with shock in their eyes.

Ralph Coates looked back at Aaron Veldon, now lying on the ground. His body twitched once and then settled into the utter finality of death.

Roy Durwood found his voice and yelled, 'What the hell did you do that for, Sally?'

'Somebody had to do it!'

'You know how I feel about killing. The man wasn't even armed. That was murder!'

'So who's going to tell that sheriff? You?' she challenged.

Carl Ranahan and Brian Quarmby raced round the corner of the house to find out what was going on, alerted by the shot sound. In stunned silence they gazed down at the lifeless rancher. At the same time a woman of middle years appeared at the front door of the house and screamed when she saw Veldon lying there. Ralph Coates dismounted and vaulted over the gates, then walked towards the stricken woman.

'I'm sorry, ma'am. It was an accident,' he lied, still confused by the sudden revelation of another side to the character of Sally Freeman. It was hard to comprehend after her compassion weeks earlier and the way she had nursed him.

'Are you Mrs Veldon?'

'No. Mrs Veldon died some years ago. I look after Mr Veldon now.' She glanced towards the corpse. 'Is he dead?'

'Afraid so, ma'am. Is there anyone else here?'

'No.' She seemed remarkably calm about the sudden demise of her employer, but Coates wondered how long her composure would hold. 'The men have all gone off to tend the cattle and things.'

'We'll bring him into the house, then when they come back they can bury him. I expect he'd want to be buried on his own land.'

'Yes,' she agreed. 'I'll get them to bury him beside his wife.'

'If you'll show me where to put him, ma'am?'

She hesitated, her eyes beginning to moisten. 'In his bedroom?'

'I think that might be the best place.'

He was thankful she did not ask who had fired the shot.

Carl Ranahan assisted Coates to carry the body, while the others shuffled uncomfortably on their mounts. When the two men came out again they both looked at Sally Freeman through fresh eyes, still scarcely able to believe that she had committed cold-blooded murder.

'Let's get out of here!' Roy Durwood commanded, agitated.

Sally Freeman and Coates exchanged glances, hers defiant, as if seeking his support. 'I did it for you, Ralph.'

'I know, but it was wrong, Sally.'

'Come on!' Durwood yelled urgently.

Coates looked at him with understanding, knowing the man had been deeply shocked by what Sally had done and wanted to protect her from being charged with murder. He forked his horse and followed Durwood's lead as the gang leader urged his steeldust into a fast lope.

They rode for twenty minutes before Durwood headed for a stand of trees that offered shade from the broiling sun. He dismounted and the others eased out of their saddles, each looking from one to the other, their equilibrium disturbed by the surprise killing of the rancher, and wondering what they were going to do about it.

'What are we gonna do, Coates?' Durwood queried.

'Your options are limited. As you said yourself back there, it was murder, so we're all in it together.'

Sally spoke up. 'I'm the one who killed him.'

Coates eyed her with indignation battling against the fact that if it had not been for her compassion weeks earlier, he might well be dead. He was still finding it hard to reconcile her obvious goodness in conflict with the cold fury she had revealed in her killing of Aaron Veldon. Did she have some kind of split personality which

113

flashed from compassion for someone in need to irrational fury when she did not get her own way? Something so simple as Veldon's refusal to admit to her accusation was too little to provoke a killing in any normal person.

She held his gaze as he considered his reply.

'Who fired the shot doesn't make a lot of difference, Sally. According to the law, the rest of us are accessories before and after the fact. We all bear the responsibility.'

'But that can't be right. Why should you suffer because of what I did?'

'It's the law, Sally. If you hang, we all hang.'

Badly shaken, she moved towards Roy Durwood. 'I'm sorry, Roy, but I just got so mad about what he'd done and he stood there just lying through his teeth. You know I'm right, don't you?'

'I guess there's not much doubt about that, but we'd never be able to prove it, unless we catch either Lou Pike or Tweedy and get one of them to admit it.'

Sally gazed around the assembled group, each of them digesting what Coates had said about the law. None of them spoke; not even to condemn her. Coates figured Durwood was battling with emotions that flitted from anger to love. He had spent three years in intimate liaison with this woman and now the unexpected turn of fortune put him in an unenviable position.

114

'You'd best make up your mind what you intend to do, Roy,' Coates reminded him.

Durwood shifted his eyes from Sally to Coates. 'Seems like we don't have too much choice. When those men get back for supper tonight, one of them will hightail it into Oak Creek and report the killing to that sheriff.'

Coates nodded. 'You're right about that.'

'Well if you think I'm gonna let Sally hang for killing that skunk, you're wrong. We're heading back into New Mexico.'

'That's what I figured you'd decide.'

Carl Ranahan spoke up. 'What about Pike and Tweedy?'

'They don't matter any more,' Durwood snapped back. 'It's ourselves we have to worry about now.'

'Something like this was bound to happen one day,' Ranahan mused aloud. 'I reckon we all knew that.'

'How about you, Ralph?' Durwood asked. 'You coming with us?'

'No, Roy, I cain't do that. Not many years back I wore a star myself, an' I've always been on the side o' the law. I don't fancy becomin' a fugitive now.'

Ranahan faced him. 'What you gonna do, Ralph?'

'Go an' see Adelman. Tell him what happened. You should be over the border before he can organise a posse.'

'You think he'd do that, him being only town sheriff?'

'From what I've heard, it was Veldon who got him appointed in the first place, but now the rancher's dead, who knows what he'll do? He could contact the Ranger Office.'

'And those Texas Rangers don't give up easily,' Arnold Glover told them.

'There'd be a price on all our heads,' Brian Quarmby said.

'Not the way I'd tell it.'

'You mean....?'

Sally moved forward to look up at Coates. 'You mean you'd say you killed that rancher?'

The girl was far too intuitive and Coates found it hard to lie to her. 'You saved my life, Sally, you and the others.'

'That's no reason for you to give it up for me now!'

He made no response and she went back to Durwood, leading him away from the group to indulge in a whispered discussion. After a while Durwood nodded in acquiescence and Sally came back to face the others, looking at each in turn.

'I'm going into Oak Creek with Ralph and tell that sheriff just what happened. I won't have the rest of you hang for what I did.'

They all protested, with the exception of Coates,

who wondered exactly what agreement had been reached between Sally and Durwood. The arguments continued until Durwood bellowed, 'She's made up her mind, fellers, so quit arguing and let's ride.'

Quarmby, Arnold Glover and Ranahan all stared back at him in silence, until understanding dawned in their minds. Coates suspected that a plan of action had been previously agreed between them long ago about what they would do if any of them were arrested, but he did not want to think about that.

Ranahan said, 'I'm staying with Ralph. We haven't finished what we started. I'll join you after we get Pike and Tweedy.'

'And how do you think you're gonna find them, Carl?' Quarmby queried disdainfully.

'They can't have gone far.'

'But you've no idea which direction they took.'

'Pike needs a doctor, Brian. Where else would he find one but El Paso?'

THIRTEEN

Herb Adelman watched their approach as he stood outside his office door, wondering why five men and one woman had left town together that morning and now only two men accompanied the woman back again.

They brought their horses to a standstill and Coates looked down at the sheriff. 'We'd like to talk t'you, Sheriff.'

'Thought you might. Take the weight off your asses and come on in.'

He turned and entered his office. By the time the three visitors had dismounted, hitched their mounts and followed him, he was sitting expectantly behind his desk. They stood hesitantly in a line.

Coates broke the silence. 'We've brought Mrs Freeman in. She has something she wants to tell you.'

Adelman held his curiosity in check with difficulty. 'Well, Mrs Freeman, what is it?'

'I've come to give myself up, Sheriff. I killed Aaron Veldon this morning.'

Astonishment registered on Adelman's face. 'Killed him! You?'

'I was pointing my gun at him, trying to get him to tell us where Lou Pike was, and the gun went off.'

'Accidentally or on purpose?'

She stared back at him with false indignation. 'Do you think I'd surrender myself if I'd shot him deliberately? I'm throwing myself on your mercy.'

The sheriff rubbed his chin thoughtfully, undecided what his response should be. He had never arrested a woman before and the idea of locking up this highly personable member of the female sex bothered him.

It also bothered Ralph Coates that he was allowing himself to be a party to passing off a blatant murder as an accident, but he felt the burden to his conscience was small when set against his indebtedness to Sally Freeman. He was just as certain in his own mind as she was that Veldon had deserved to die.

'Can you confirm this shooting was an accident, Coates?'

'I heard the shot an' saw Veldon fall, Sheriff. I wasn't lookin' in Mrs Freeman's direction at the time.'

Adelman focussed his attention on Carl Ranahan. 'How about you, mister?'

'I was round by the bunkhouse when it happened. I saw nothing but the dead man lying on the ground.'

The sheriff scratched his head in bewilderment, then said, 'It seems to me, Mrs Freeman, you're a mite short of witnesses to corroborate your claim that this shooting was accidental. By your own admission you were threatening Mr Veldon with a gun.'

'Just trying to scare him into telling us what we needed to know, Sheriff.'

Coates defended her. 'Mrs Freeman is quite prepared to go on trial for this unfortunate incident, Sheriff.'

Adelman eyed Sally again, contemplating his options, and finding he didn't have any. 'In that case, Mrs Freeman, I'll have to hold you, pending an investigation. I'm sorry.'

'No need to apologise, Sheriff. I expected that.'

He stood up and reached for the cell door keys. 'If you'd come this way, please.'

The two men standing either side of Sally could see Adelman was acutely embarrassed by the need to lock her up. They both followed and were allowed to say their goodbyes while Adelman returned to the front office.

Before they left, Coates told Adelman, 'We'd be obliged if you'd let her have anything she needs, Sheriff, an' a visit from Liz Perry. We'll leave her horse down at the livery.'

'No problem. Where will you be?'

'On the trail of Lou Pike an' Keith Tweedy. We'll be back.'

When they got outside and remounted Carl Ranahan grinned at Coates. 'Seems like he forgot he wanted to talk to me about last night.'

'I reckon he's real put out at havin' t'lock up a woman as pretty as Sally.'

Liz Perry was shocked by the news Coates imparted, but she readily agreed to pay visits to the jailhouse to see Sally Freeman. 'Such an elegant young lady,' she mused aloud in bewilderment.

She looked into Coates' blue eyes again. 'Does this mean you'll be leaving us right away?'

'It does, but we'll be back.'

Her face clouded with concern. 'I do hope so, Ralph. You, too, Mr Ranahan.'

Ranahan flashed her the smile that had melted

many a woman's heart, and even in his late forties was still potent. 'I'll look forward to that, ma'am.'

They camped near the old burnt-out homestead, Ranahan wondering if Coates was being morbid in selecting that particular spot.

'The old well still works, I reckon,' Coates said by way of explanation, 'an' I can sure use some coffee.'

It made sense and Ranahan accepted that Coates was being practical rather than wanting to dwell on his failure to protect Consuela Martinez. That it would be in his mind was not in doubt. Coates would probably never fully rid himself of that burden on his conscience, even after she had been avenged. He guessed it was not the only weight on the fair-haired man's mind.

After they had eaten the beef and bread Liz Perry had supplied and drained their coffee mugs, Ranahan said, 'What happens after we get those two, Ralph?'

'I guess it'll be time for me to head back to Arizona. I've gotten unfinished business there. Not seen my folks for three years now, either.'

'And what about us? Roy and the rest of us?'

'How d'you mean?'

'You said you'd once been a badge toter. You intend to turn a blind eye?'

Coates tilted his head. 'I cain't condone the way

123

you make your livin', Carl, but I reckon I owe you, an' I've no evidence of any robberies you've been involved in. I hope we'll part with a handshake, but after that I don't ever want to see you or any of the gang again.' After a brief silence he felt the need to qualify the statement. 'If you should decide to quit robbin' banks an' settle down to ranch work, I'd be glad to have you with me.'

'You got a ranch back in Arizona, Ralph?'

'I had a share in one before....'

Ranahan waited for him to finish what he had started to say, but he didn't. 'Before your wife died?' he prompted.

'Yeah.'

'You reckon your partner will want you back?'

'Mebbe not, but it's just possible. I'm goin' back there because I owe him at least an explanation.'

There seemed to be nothing more to say and the two men became enclosed by silence, watching the sun descend to bring another day to an end.

No words were spoken, but as if by common consent, they eventually spread their bedrolls and settled down for the night. Both men were well practised in closing their minds to the events of the day and they were soon asleep.

FOURTEEN

Through the waves of weakness ebbing and flowing, his muscles stabbing painfully in protest at the prolonged ride, Lou Pike lost some of his resolve to survive. Aching, tired limbs can make the mind grow sluggish, soon to be persuaded that nothing matters any more. Even slight effort becomes no longer worthwhile. Swaying in the saddle, he would have crashed to the ground had not Keith Tweedy been riding close alongside and able to grab his right arm.

'You wanna rest, Lou?' he asked as he drew rein.

Pike's reply was indistinguishable.

'It's only a few more miles, Lou, then that sawbones'll fix you up. Can you make it?'

Tweedy had the feeling that if Pike left the saddle he would never climb up again. He eased himself out of his stirrups and tied Pike's hands to his saddlehorn. Pike's chin rested on his chest, his eyes were closed and he seemed barely conscious, all his earlier bravado and determination to get himself healed and then go after Ralph Coates again dissipated by the constant, throbbing pain in his left shoulder. Tweedy, so long attached to the sadistic killer that he could not contemplate the future without him, was resolved to get him to El Paso.

They arrived in the shank of the day and Tweedy hammered on the door of the doctor's abode.

'What in tarnation are you makin' all that racket for?' the doctor's wife demanded as she opened the door.

'Lou is hurt bad!' Tweedy snapped back. 'He needs the doc!'

'Oh, all right. You'd best bring him in then. You'll have to wait until he finishes his supper. Sit there.' She indicated the long seat in the hallway, then disappeared through one of the doors off to the right.

The aroma of cooking penetrated the hallway, reminding Keith Tweedy that he had not eaten

126

since morning. His belly rumbled at thoughts of food and he determined to eat as soon as he'd gotten Lou Pike fixed up. No sense in allowing himself to grow weak through hunger. He needed to maintain his strength if he was to take care of Pike until he was his old self again.

Dr Travers came out a few minutes later and looked briefly at the limp frame of Lou Pike, being supported by the much larger Keith Tweedy. 'Bring him in here.'

Tweedy lifted Pike as if he was no heavier than a baby and followed the doctor into his surgery.

'Put him on the couch. Tell me what happened.'

'He took a bullet in the shoulder last night, Doc. He didn't bleed all that much but I reckon enough to weaken him. He's been in powerful pain.'

Travers removed Pike's shirt, while Tweedy supported him.

'H'mm. I'll have to clean him up before I can see what the damage is. Where did this shooting take place?'

'Oak Creek, in the Mulehead Saloon.'

Pike's head lolled towards his right shoulder, his brain dulled to accept whatever happened to him. When Travers had cleared away the dried blood and surveyed the wound he said, 'That's a bad one. The bullet has clipped the collar bone. Splintered it. It will take a long time to heal.'

'You can help him, Doc?'

127

'Not much, I'm afraid. Only time and the growth of new tissue will make him feel less pain. He'll never be the same again. That arm won't be much use to him for a long time. I can put a dressing on the torn flesh and give him a better sling for the arm, but that's about all. Have you anywhere to take him close by?'

'No, Doc. I'll have to get us a room some place.'

'Best leave him here while you go and do that.'

'Right, Doc. Be back as soon as I can.'

Roy Durwood found his nerves getting frayed as he waited with Arnold Glover and Brian Quarmby in El Paso. He worried over the fact that they had not crossed the border line into New Mexico, but he was even more anxious to have news of Sally.

Quarmby edged into the saloon and headed towards the table where the other two were seated, each with a beer at his hand.

'Any sign?' Durwood snapped.

'No, but I've just seen that big feller who was with those other two when we were at that homestead.'

'That'll be Tweedy.'

Glover said, 'So Carl was right. They did come here to see that sawbones.'

'We're no longer concerned about Tweedy and Pike,' Durwood reminded them. 'All we're waiting here for is to find out what happened to Sal in Oak

Creek.'

'But Carl is,' Quarmby argued. 'If we can help Carl and Coates, don't you think we owe it to them?'

'I told you, all I'm concerned about is Sal. Now get back out there and keep watch. They should be here by now!'

'I could use a drink, Roy. It's hot out there.'

'I'll go,' Glover offered. 'You get yourself a beer, Brian.'

Coates and Ranahan would have agreed with Quarmby. Their shirts were sticking to their backs as they rode into El Paso and saw Glover standing outside the saloon, a grin of welcome on his face. No one could ever call what passed for a smile on Glover's face anything but a grin.

'I'm sure glad t'see you two,' he said. 'Roy's become a pain, waiting for news about Sally. You fellers wanna drink?'

'Is a Catholic Father a priest?' Ranahan replied with heavy sarcasm. 'Lead me to it, Arnold.'

'Brian saw that big feller here in town a while back,' Glover informed them as they slid from their saddles and hitched the horses to the tie rail.

Ranahan and Coates exchanged smiles of satisfaction.

'So you didn't cross over into New Mexico,' Coates said after they were all seated around the same table and he had taken a pull on his beer.

'Did you think we'd run out on Sally?' Durwood challenged.

Coates weighed the question before answering. 'I guess not. Well you can rest easy for a while. Adelman was a mite put out when Sally offered to stand trial. I reckon it'll be hard for a jury to convict her, especially if you stay away from the trial. No use lettin' yourselves get called as witnesses if you want to see her get away with it.'

'Get away with it?'

The gaze Coates fixed on Durwood was scornful. His voice was quiet. 'Don't play games with me, Roy. If I didn't owe my life to you all I wouldn't be a party to coverin' up plain murder.'

'Don't you think Veldon instructed those men to teach you a lesson and make an example of you to others?'

'Yes, I do, but we've no proof. As a former sheriff I deal in facts that will hold up in a court o' law, not conjecture. When Adelman asked me to corroborate what Sally told him I prevaricated. It don't sit easy on my mind, but I'll live with it because I owe her an' I do believe she was right in her thinkin'. I'm just as convinced as she is that Aaron Veldon was as guilty of killin' Consuela as the man who fired the shots.'

Durwood's eyes shifted to Ranahan. 'You were right, Carl. Those two killers did come to El Paso.'

'Where are they now?'

'We don't know.'

Ranahan looked hard at Quarmby. 'Why didn't you follow Tweedy when you spotted him?'

'How did you ...' His eyes swivelled to take in Glover. 'So you told them.'

Sheepishly Glover answered, 'Any reason why I shouldn't?'

'I guess not.'

Ranahan turned his attention back to Coates. 'We could pay Doc Travers a visit, Ralph. He might know.'

'He might, but I doubt he'd tell us.'

Ranahan drained his glass and stood up. 'Let's go and find out. See you fellers later,' he said to the others.

'Have you treated a scruffy looking little man for a gunshot wound, Doc, either yesterday or today?'

'Whom I treat and for what is no concern of yours and you should know better than to ask, Mr Ranahan.'

The voice of Doctor Travers had a bite to it that the big man could hardly ignore, but he persisted. 'We have reason to believe that man is not only guilty of murder but also of another attempted murder, Doc.'

'That is not my concern, Mr Ranahan. That is a matter for the law. I suggest you go and see the county sheriff.'

'He is also the man who was responsible for that terrible whipping that was inflicted on Ralph Coates, or doesn't that cut any ice with you?'

Coates had elected to allow Ranahan to speak to the medic alone, remaining outside the house at a discreet distance. He knew by the tight expression on his partner's face roughly what the outcome of the interview had been when Ranahan rejoined him.

'Did he plead confidentiality, Carl?'

'Exactly as you said he would. But we'll find them. I figure Pike will still need treatment, so he's not planning to leave El Paso yet awhile.'

'We could visit the county sheriff an' tell him about the killin' of Consuela.'

Ranahan scoffed. 'Ain't you forgetting something?'

'What?'

'Evidence to put in front of a jury. We know who killed her but *we can't prove it.*'

FIFTEEN

Lou Pike opened his eyes and looked up as Keith Tweedy returned to their room. Tweedy's customary smiling countenance was not in evidence and Pike knew something was wrong.

'What is it, Keith? What's worryin' you?'

'Coates and that big feller are in town. I've just seen them. I guess they're looking for us.'

'Did they see you?'

'No. I ducked back out of sight as soon as I spotted them.'

Pike propped himself up on his good elbow, frowning. 'Won't take 'em long t'find us if we stay here.'

'What we gonna do, Lou? You're in no state to face Coates right now.'

Weakened by the constant pain which still plagued him, Pike was obliged to agree. 'We gotta get out o' here.'

'We can't go out now, Lou. They might see us.'

'We'll wait 'til it gets dark, then head across the border into New Mexico. I know a place we can hide for a spell. Best get some rest, Keith, if we're gonna ride all night.'

'We're lookin' for a friend of ours,' Ralph Coates told the hotel keeper. 'Wondered if he might be stayin' here. Big feller with long hair. Always smilin'. Name of Tweedy. Keith Tweedy?'

'Nobody by that name here.'

The hotel man recognised the description of the man these two strangers were looking for, but he had signed the register as Graham Pyne. The sick man with him called himself Fowler. His instincts told the hotel keeper that these two tall men were not being entirely truthful in describing Graham Pyne, or Keith Tweedy, if indeed it was him, as a friend. He had a nose for this kind of subterfuge, having experienced it to his cost in the past. He was not anxious for trouble in his hotel. Both these men looked as if they could handle their holstered guns with some skill and he had an aversion to bullets flying around. Violent death was repellent to him.

'Why don't you try the rooming house down the street?' he suggested, his belly knotted with fear.

'We'll do that, mister,' Ranahan said with a smile. 'Thanks for your time.'

Outside again, Ranahan asked Coates, 'You think he was telling the truth?'

'Hard to say, but he did seem kinda nervous.'

Back inside, the hotel man waited until he saw Coates and Ranahan move off down the street, then he went up the stairs and knocked softly on a bedroom door. When Tweedy opened it he was told, 'Two men asking about you, Mr Pyne, only they said your name was Tweedy.'

Not a subtle man, Tweedy asked, 'Was one a big feller with corn-coloured hair?'

'He was. Said he was a friend o' yours but I figured he might've been lying.'

'You were right. He's no friend. Was the other man older, grey beard?'

'Indeed he was.'

'What did you tell these men?'

'Said you weren't here. Told 'em to try the rooming house down the street. I didn't want no trouble.'

'Thanks.'

The hotel man nodded and turned away as Tweedy closed the door.

'You hear that, Lou? That Coates is looking for us.'

'Yeah, I heard. Go down an' pay our tab, an' give that man some extra for keepin' his mouth shut. Tell him we'll be leavin' after sundown.'

His left shoulder still aching but eased by the sling that held his left arm bent at the elbow, taking the weight, Lou Pike walked cautiously alongside Keith Tweedy as they made their way to the livery stables. They walked along the back lots, avoiding the main street. The sounds of raucous laughter from one of the saloons was louder than their footfalls and there were few men on the street to their right. They edged in through the livery doors and in the light of the single lantern illuminating the stables, Tweedy saddled their horses, then helped Pike climb aboard his buckskin.

The big man led both horses out into the street before mounting himself, too anxious to put El Paso behind him to notice the two men who had crossed the street while he and Pike were inside and were now patiently waiting at the side of the stables. In the dim light showing through the open doors, Ralph Coates and Carl Ranahan stepped out, guns in their hands.

'That's far enough, Pike, Tweedy. You're under arrest,' Coates barked.

Stunned by the sudden appearance of the two men, Pike and Tweedy stared back aghast. Then

Tweedy found his voice.

'You ain't no lawman, Coates!'

Ignoring the challenge, Coates said, 'We're takin' you back to Oak Creek to stand trial for murder.'

'Like hell you are!' Pike snarled, his fury and frustration overcoming his sense of weakness and, whipping his gun from its holster, he began firing in one swift movement.

In the near darkness Coates did not see the blur of Pike's hand quick enough and this time the gunman's bullet found its mark. Coates fired as he spun around from the impact of the lead slug, but his shot flew into thin air. Ranahan loosed off two quick shots, but the horses reared and screamed their fear of the close proximity to shot sound and took flight. Neither of Ranahan's bullets had found the target, but one of them furrowed a deep burn mark on the left flank of Tweedy's mount.

With only one arm of any use to him, his right hand fisting his gun, the buckskin's reins hanging loose, Lou Pike fought to stay in the saddle, feet held hard in the stirrups and knees gripping his mount's belly, but he was fighting a losing battle. Halfway up the street he lost his balance and toppled, one foot still trapped awkwardly in a stirrup, his head bumping on the hard-baked ground. The pain in his shoulder as he repeatedly bounced along the street was excruciating and by

137

the time the buckskin eased down to a halt he had fainted.

He came to as Tweedy lifted him and ran into an alley. The big man stood him down and, crouching, held him around the waist. 'You hurt bad, Lou?'

'He didn't hit me, but my shoulder ...' Pike whispered agonizingly.

'Can you cope while I get the horses back?'

'Yeah, you do that. We gotta get outa here.'

Coates was on his knees, fighting the pain that swept through him. He was aware of men running and Carl Ranahan bending over him.

'Where are you hit, Ralph?'

'Chest. I'll be all right in a minute. Did you get either of 'em, Carl?'

'Reckon not. The horses reared and fled just as I fired. Let me give you a hand, I'll get you to the doc.'

By the time Coates was on his feet they were surrounded with curious onlookers. One of them spoke up.

'What's all the ruckus about? Who fired all those shots?'

Ranahan looked up and noticed the star on the man's coat as the stable light fell dimly on the tin.

'Are you the county sheriff?'

'I am. Who are you?'

138

'Carl Ranahan. I was helping Mr Coates here to effect a citizen's arrest. Two men responsible for killing a Mexican woman six or seven weeks back.'

'Citizen's arrest, huh? Arrestin' killers is my job, Ranahan. How come you didn't acquaint me of this killin'?'

Ranahan thought fast. 'You were out of town when we called at your office, Sheriff.'

The lawman grunted. 'I've gotten a big bailiwick.'

'I know that. That's why, when we found Pike and Tweedy trying to sneak out of town, we tried to stop them.'

'Hit either o' them?'

'Don't think so, but Pike is a wounded man. Shot a couple of nights back when he tried to kill Mr Coates in Oak Creek. He came here to get medical help.'

Another voice piped up. 'Two horses loose on the street back there, Sheriff. Could be their mounts.'

'Come with me, men. If those two are still in town I'd like to talk to them.'

After they had gone, Ranahan helped Coates in the direction of Doctor Travers' house.

'I guess it's out of our hands now, Carl.'

'Depends if that sheriff finds them.'

It had taken Tweedy several minutes to reacquaint himself with the two horses and lead them

139

back to where he had left Lou Pike. As they were on the point of remounting they were alerted by the approach of the sheriff and his hastily appointed posse.

'Hey! You there! Don't make another move, you're under arrest!'

'Oh, no, we ain't,' Pike whispered to Tweedy, finding enough stength to move back into the shadows, away from the horses. Pike drew his gun again, firing until the chamber was empty.

Tweedy, unaccustomed to the use of guns, was shocked into immobility by his pard's fierce reluctance to surrendering to the law and failed to back him up. The two of them slumped to the street under a hail of bullets fired by the sheriff and his helpers. Pike had managed to wound two of them before he died.

When the gunsmoke cleared the sheriff moved forward, reloading his pistol.

He gazed down at the still bodies, while other men picked up the fallen guns of the fugitives. Kneeling down, he felt for a pulse, first Pike and then Tweedy. He pronounced them both dead.

'Get these men back to my office, fellers. I'll get the doc to certify death in the mornin'. Right now I want to talk t'those other two.'

'We've gotten two casualties, Sheriff,' he was told.

'Get 'em over to the doc's place then. And

140

thanks for your help, fellers.'

'Unfeelin' bastard!' one of the wounded men muttered, but if the sheriff heard him he gave no sign. He was well known as a hard man.

SIXTEEN

'Well, Coates, you got what you wanted without getting blood on your hands,' Roy Durwood said the following morning. 'You must be pleased about that. You'd never have gotten those two into a court room. Circumstances sure pointed to their being guilty of your friend's murder but no hard evidence.'

'Life is full of ironies, don't you find, Roy?'

'I guess so.'

Ironic last night's events had certainly proved. The law had dealt out justice in an unexpected manner, leaving Coates and Ranahan free from any possible charges of unlawful killing. The bearded man had expressed his relief earlier to Coates.

Durwood said, 'Well I guess this is goodbye. We've gotten Sally to think about now. You coming, Carl?'

'No, Roy, I'm staying with Ralph.'

The gang leader's face registered disappointment. 'Coates don't need you to nurse him through this one, Carl. Didn't the doc say his wound was clean? He'll be as good as new in six weeks, you told me.'

'I know. I'm quitting, Roy.'

'Quitting!' Durwood found Ranahan's decision hard to believe. 'After all we've been through together? You can't.'

'Sorry, Roy, but I'm getting too old for all that excitement we've had. When Ralph goes back to Arizona I'm going with him.'

'To do what?'

Ranahan shrugged. 'To give whatever help he needs. Ranching.'

'You! You couldn't rope a steer if your life depended on it.'

'I'm not too old to learn.'

'And what about the years we've been together? Don't they count any more?'

'Sure they do, but like I said, I'm getting too old for all that travel. You're nigh on twenty years younger than me.'

Durwood stood and gazed at him through a long silence, reluctant to accept that his closest friend was deserting him.

Then Ranahan said, 'When you get to my age – if you ever do – I guess you'll feel like settling down some place.'

Listening to the exchanges, Ralph Coates had a strong suspicion that Durwood was heading for an early grave if he persisted in his life outside the law. He didn't need telling that was Ranahan's line of thinking.

Durwood's gaze was scornful. 'Well I sure won't end my days working my butt on some ranch.' With an exasperated sigh he added, 'If you change your mind, you know where to find us. S'long, Carl. Been nice knowing you, Coates.'

Coates was fairly sure that was not quite the truth. He'd been more of a nuisance as far as Roy Durwood was concerned, irked by Sally Freeman's decision to nurse him after the whipping and Carl's change of allegiance.

When Durwood had gone, Coates said, 'You sure you know what you're getting into, Carl?'

'No, but I know what I'm getting out of and I've enough money to tide me over for a year, I reckon.'

It didn't seem to bother him that the money he had put by was the proceeds of bank raids, and Coates decided to turn a blind eye to that. At least the man was prepared to give up robbery.

* * *

Sheriff Adelman raised no objections when Roy Durwood asked if he could visit Sally. He was curious about the visitor but he had no knowledge of how the gang leader made his living. Besides, the man was the prisoner's husband, so what was more natural than that he would want to visit her? The fact that he was alone eased any suspicions Adelman might have entertained if the other men had accompanied him to the jailhouse. The woman had surrendered herself and was prepared to go on trial for the killing of Aaron Veldon, so what had he got to worry about? What puzzled him was why Durwood had not been with his wife when she surrendered herself. Why had he left it to Ralph Coates and that Ranahan to accompany her?

'Trial is tomorrow, Mr Freeman.'

'I'll be there, Sheriff.'

The advice Ralph Coates had given him on that point could safely be ignored. It would be far more suspicious if he absented himself.

'You know if that Coates feller will be in court to give evidence, Mr Freeman?'

'I guess not, Sheriff. He was shot in El Paso two nights ago.'

Adelman's eyes opened wider. 'Dead?'

'No. Clean chest wound, as I understand it.'

146

'Pity. I'd have liked to have him in court as a witness.' He pushed out a sigh. 'Oh, well, I'd best take you through to see your wife.'

She had missed him enormously and his dark good looks and winning smile could still make her heart lurch. 'How are you, Sal? They been looking after you all right?'

Her eyes lit up with delight. 'Sure, Roy. I've no complaints. That Mrs Perry has been in each day to make sure I'm getting properly fed. How are things with you and the boys?'

'Carl has left us. Going to Arizona with Coates.'

Her surprise was total, in spite of knowing how incensed Carl had been about what had happened to Coates. 'Really?' The two men must have become close during his recuperation.

'Yeah. The two of them got lucky in their chase after Pike and that Tweedy feller.'

And he proceeded to tell her what had happened in El Paso.

'I'm glad about that. Carl is getting too old to spend time in jail. I expect that's why he's decided to go with Ralph to Arizona. He'll find it hard though, ranching, after the easy life he's led with you all these years.'

Durwood pushed Ranahan from his mind and concentrated on the immediate future. 'Trial's tomorrow, the sheriff tells me.'

147

'It might not be as easy for me to get off as we first thought, Roy. The foreman back at Veldon's ranch will be in court, asking for a guilty verdict.'

'What does he know about it? He wasn't there!'

'Sheriff says I don't have a witness to say my gun went off accidentally.'

'He don't have one to say otherwise, either.'

Sally was no longer smiling. 'If things don't go my way, Roy, will you....?'

'Sure we will. Don't you worry, Sal. They can't hang a woman. I'll not let them.'

Somebody had persuaded Aaron Veldon's housekeeper to testify that Sally Freeman had shot her employer in cold blood. She claimed to have been looking out of a window when Sally drew her gun and fired the shot. Roy Durwood couldn't help thinking she'd been got at in some way. Maybe her future depended on it. She might not have had a lot of respect for Veldon and she would not grieve for his passing, but finding herself unemployed at her time of life would offer her a bleak future.

The prosecution had hired the only lawyer in Oak Creek, and Roy Durwood had been unable to find anyone willing to represent Sally. She had only her own words with which to defend herself. They were not enough. Veldon had been far more popular than Roy Durwood had imagined and it

seemed the whole town was against Sally, most of
them wanting a guilty verdict.

They got it, but the circuit judge was reluctant
to have the hanging of a woman on his conscience.
He spoke at length about women who carried
firearms in public places and the risks they faced
in so doing. 'Fortunately for you, as far as the
court has been able to ascertain, you are a woman
of previously good character, but you are
undoubtedly guilty of an unlawful killing of one of
Oak Creek's most respected citizens and you will
spend twenty years in prison,' he announced at
the conclusion of his reasoning.

The banging of his gavel sounded to Sally like
the death knell. She looked at Roy Durwood with
pleading eyes as Sheriff Adelman led her away to
await transportation to the prison.

It was close to midnight and even activities in the
Mulehead Saloon were winding down. Only a few
men remained, playing out their last hands, and
the women had retired for the night. At the poker
table Brian Quarmby was on a winning streak,
watched by a smiling Arnold Glover. The other
players were not amused and gradually all but
one threw in his hand. The remaining punter
tried to bluff his way for three more calls before
asking to see what Quarmby was holding. He
snorted in disgust and toppled his chair over

149

backwards as he stood up.

'You've gotten the luck o' the devil, mister!'

'Your turn tomorrow, maybe.'

Quarmby drew the pot towards him and dispersed it in two different pockets. Moments later only he and Glover remained in the saloon. They eyed each other without smiling, knowing the task that awaited them outside. They said goodnight to the apron and made for the door.

Roy Durwood was waiting for them opposite the jailhouse by earlier arrangement.

'Any problems, Roy?' Quarmby queried.

'Adelman has a deputy playing jailor. We should be able to handle him easily enough.'

'Where are the horses?'

'Hitched behind Perrys Hotel. Let's get on with it.'

He looked up and down the street, saw that it was deserted, and led the way to the other side and up to the jailhouse door. The other two stood aside as he knocked softly.

'Who is it?' a voice called from inside.

'Texas Ranger! Open up!' Durwood called, disguising his voice as best he could.

The three men heard the bar being removed and a key turning in the lock as they pulled bandannas up to cover their faces. As soon as the door opened just a few inches Durwood barged his way inside, knocking the deputy off balance.

150

Before he could scramble to his feet, Durwood had his gun pointing at the deputy's head.

'Now just you act sensible and you won't get hurt.'

'You won't get away with this, mister.'

'Not much you can do about it right now. Up on your feet, get me that woman's gun and belt and the cell door key.'

Complying with the instruction, the deputy feared for his own skin, wondering if they intended killing him after they'd freed the woman. He led the way to where Sally Freeman was locked in, stood aside while Durwood opened the cell door and handed the gunbelt and weapon to her, then watched as she strapped the belt around her hips, smiling as she did so.

'Sorry to have to leave you, Deputy, but I'm too fond of fresh air to go off to that prison.'

She stepped out into the corridor and Durwood motioned the deputy to take her place. As the man stepped through the door Durwood clipped him lightly with his gun barrel, watching as he slumped to the floor.

'Grab your coat from the office and let's be on our way, Sal. Won't be long before he surfaces, I reckon.'

SEVENTEEN

Sheriff Herb Adelman heard the bawling of his deputy when he returned to his office the next morning, after a night with his woman down the street. His good humour promptly turned sour.

He went through to the back and stared in dismay. 'What the hell happened?'

The deputy, shame-faced, nervously explained.

'Dammit, Jepson, they'll be more'n half way to the border by now!' Adelman bellowed as he unlocked the cell door.

'How was I to know it wasn't that Ranger who was here last year? It sure sounded like his voice.'

'What in tarnation did you think Captain Buck

would be doing calling at the jailhouse at midnight?'

'I'm sorry, Sheriff. I guess I let you down.'

'And not just me; the whole town wanted to see that woman taken off to prison. If I were you, Jepson, I'd hightail it to El Paso before the news gets all around town.'

'I ain't had no breakfast, Sheriff!' Jepson complained.

'Which is most important, getting lynched or feeding your face?'

'Lynched! They wouldn't do that to me!'

'No?' Adelman's cold stare was enough to convince Jepson of the possibility.

He went through to the front office, grabbed his hat, coat and gunbelt, then shot out of the door without a backward glance.

Adelman muttered through an exasperated sigh, 'And I thought Jepson had brains. The only thing his head is good for is a hatstand.'

The most galling aspect of the situation as far as the sheriff was concerned dwelt in the fact that he himself had chosen Jepson to act as jailor, and he would have to share the blame for the prisoner's escape. He flounced out of his office and headed for the telegraph office in a hurry. At least he could get a message off to the Ranger Headquarters and ask for help in recapturing Sally Freeman and the men who had freed her. It must have been that husband of hers and some of his friends. Not that he held out any hope. If they were smart enough to free the woman they would surely have sense enough to get out of Texas and never come back.

It was three days later that news of the jailbreak reached El Paso. Carl Ranahan heard of it as he sat having a thirst-quencher in that same saloon where he and Ralph Coates had rejoined Roy Durwood and the other two members of his gang some days ago. It came as no surprise to him: in fact he would have gambled on it if the trial had gone against Sally. Obviously it had.

He went back to the hotel where Coates was resting his wounded chest and informed him of what he had heard.

'Does that mean Sally was found guilty, you think?' Coates queried.

'I guess it does. If she'd been acquitted there'd have been no need for a breakout. I knew they'd go in for her if things didn't go her way.'

'Must make you thankful you weren't with 'em. They'll be wanted men by now, Carl, an' Sally a wanted woman. I did warn you that something would go wrong one day. Nobody's luck lasts for ever.'

'I knew you were right, Ralph. That's why I quit the gang and elected to ride with you. How soon do you think you'll be fit to leave?'

'You worried, Carl?'

'I wouldn't want the county sheriff to connect me with Roy when he hears about this breakout.'

'But you were here with me the whole time. How could he make a charge against you?'

Ranahan upbraided himself. Shrugging, he said, 'I guess I still see myself as a part of that family, Ralph. And we were like a family.' He sighed. 'I did warn Roy that Sally would lead us into trouble one day. He didn't want to know.'

A long silence closed around them as Ranahan went and stood by the window, looking out onto the street.

Coates ruminated on Sally Freeman's future as an outlaw's woman. There was so much good in her, and yet she had elected to tie herself to a man who was nothing more than a habitual bank robber: a man who would surely die in a gun battle one day when plans did not run smoothly.

For a long time he languished in cobwebbed sadness, painfully aware of a wasted life. And yet, had it not been for Sally Freeman and her family – as Carl had called the gang – he would not be lying there, recuperating. He would have died under the scorching rays of a Texas sun weeks ago. He feared she would be wiped out before long, together with her common-law husband. It was small consolation to realize that they had escaped capture for now and were most likely well beyond the Texas border.

He looked up as Carl Ranahan turned back to face him.

'The sooner I get you to Arizona the better, Carl. Thank your lucky star you're giving yourself a chance to die in bed.'

'You gotten the dismals all of a sudden?'

'Yeah. I reckon Roy an' Sally are likely to die with their boots on.'

'I guess there's nothing we can do about that.'

He turned away once more, understanding how Coates had been feeling.

Coates recalled the promise he had made to both Sheriff Adelman and Liz Perry to return to Oak Creek, a promise he now knew he would not keep. Sally Freeman's fate had already been settled without his evidence at her trial, so there seemed little point in a return trip. He would write to Liz and Gilbert Perry after he was back home in Arizona. The immediate future was more important. He had only a vague notion of what that would hold for him and Carl, but they would face it together, bonded by events that had been forced upon them.

At least there was one heartening aspect to come out of the whole sorry episode – a former bank robber had opted for a life on the right side of the law.